THE WEEDS OF GOD

ROBERT W. WOOD

Omonomany
Memphis

Published by

Omonomany

5050 Poplar Avenue, Suite 1510

Memphis, TN 38157

(901) 374-9027 • Fax (901) 374-0508

Email jimweeks12@msn.com

Cover and art by Robert W. Wood

LCCN 2004109937

ISBN 1-59096-003-3

123456789

Printed in the United States of America

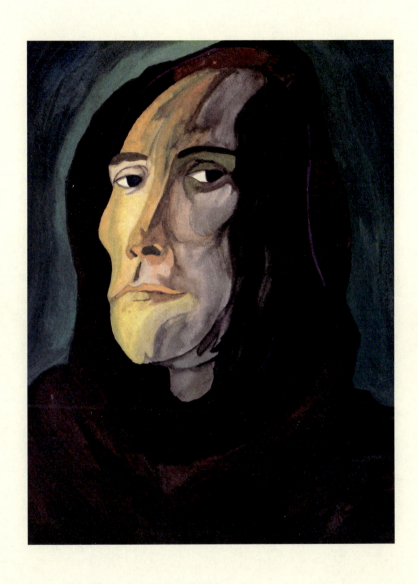

MANY SEARCH

FOR THE

MEANING OF LIFE

BUT

A FEW

GIVE LIFE MEANING

AND

IN SO DOING

FIND THE ANSWER

ELEVATORS TO EMPLOYMENT

The building looks depressed and sags in the middle like a horse ridden long and hard. It is well aware that it serves as an aquarium for state mental health patients and their mentors.

No one asks me what I want when I walk in, and no one looks particularly insane. The receptionist has a battle going with a large amount of bubble gum. "Can you tell me where Dr. Mondriatus' office is located?" I ask in my most doctor-like voice. "Fifth floor," she responds and continues to forget I exist as she engages in guerilla warfare with her double-bubble. Masticate for Jesus and be damned you daughter of a harlot.

The elevator is in no hurry in its leisurely tour of vertical possibilities. It contains a list of rules that start at the bottom of the elevator and run around its sides and beyond into the limitless depths of the elevator shaft. On the third floor, a man in a white coat with a stethoscope and a goat's head under his left arm gets on. "People claiming to be goats are ridiculous," he states and holds the stethoscope to the goat's head. "I know this because I am a psychiatrist, and dang well trained to recognize goat shit when I see it, if you catch my drift." "I am an entomologist and a Rosicrucian myself, and I like your shoes," I state while grinding my heel into the toe of his shoe. "I get your drift and you will go far in these climes if I'm not much mistaken," says he and gets off at four. The goat's head has not spoken, but we have made a silent bond, and I am sad to see him go.

The door opens at five and a slight gray fog swirls into the elevator from the waiting room. The room contains signs in twenty-six languages signed by the Paraclete of Pittsburgh. To my right there is a large stop sign and beneath the sign is a large button. I press the button and a gong sounds twice in the distance. There is a window in the door and I can see far down the hall. A herd of elephants is playing in a stream that meanders through the corridors of their minds. Two women suddenly appear at the door. One of them looks closely into my eyes and the other takes a Polaroid picture. I would like to have one with the elephants, but I am new and uncertain in my steps. The door opens. "Quickly, quickly, young doctor," states the one with the camera, "Dr. Mondriatus awaits." Come quick bwana, witch doctor makum juju.

We run swiftly down the hall to a rounded archway. Both acolytes in their white robes curtsey at the door and weave a circle thrice before the short one states, "The young one has come unto thee, Dr. Mondriatus." They disappear into the mist rising from the stream that meanders through their minds.

I walk slowly into a dim room. There are two men in the room. One sits behind a huge desk carved in the shape of a watermelon with elephant tusks for legs. He is large and seems comfortable with his largeness. A small man who looks like a cheap cigar come to life, stands in the corner under a street lamp. He is holding a sign that says, *We are not interested in any new opinio*ns. I immediately pull out a sign stating, *Free the Enigmas*. He nods wisely and winks.

On the wall is a poster. On the poster is a picture of a man with Hispanic features crouched in a dark tunnel with a bright light at the end and the faint image of a freight train. The copy at the bottom of the poster reads *Stop Illegal Transmigration*.

"Why have you applied for this job?" asks Dr. Mondriatus. This is a complex issue, but I prefer to keep the whole thing simple. "I recently graduated as you can see, and I need employment to feed the mouths of my twelve hungry children and my beloved wife, Castratus."

Dr. Mondriatus studies this answer and then types it on a 3 x 5 index card and puts it in his pocket. There is a large wart sitting just to the right of Dr. Mondriatus' very large nose. The wart is looking at me and smiling. "Are you looking at my large wart?" asks Dr. Mondriatus as he fingers his large wart. The small cigar man shakes his head vigorously and frowns. "Yes, it's a real beauty," I reply. "Good, good, I like those qualities in a psychologist."

"I really have no experience working with this type of patient except in my residency," I coyly state. "Good, good, that is exactly what we need in this damn place and you know a great wart when you see one, too," states Dr. Mondriatus. Then he begins to shift through a pile of charts on his desk while lighting a cigarette and humming something from Wagner. The small cigar man puts a disk of Lili Marlene on the turntable and returns to his street lamp.

I SING THE ELEVATOR ELECTRIC

I sing the elevator electric and breathe life into my dying psyche. The elevator and I are traveling slowly towards the light. On the third floor, a man with a pith helmet and the insignia of Her Majesty's Own Welsh Guards appears on the elevator to sing with me. "I'm extremely put out with Lord Cardigan," he states. I really could not agree more, but I am uncertain of his rank and remain silent.

"You seem to be doing well for yourself, young man, if I am to be any judge of such things," he states and withdraws a tiny pocket knife from his vest. He cuts a small nick in his thumb. "Must never be drawn without tasting blood, you know. I must advise you that this place is full of madmen, cads and charlatans. It will serve you well for you have much yet to learn, young Ashton. Have you read F. H. Bradley?" I reply in the affirmative. "Pity, everything should be read by everyone,but everything should not be read before you have reached its time, you see. Well, whatever," and he strides off the elevator to the tune of "God Save the Queen and Whatever."

I enter the unit to the sound of the ever present gong even though I now have the great keys of the kingdom. I have come to bow before Mr. Edgars, the unit administrator. His office is right next to Dr. Mondriatus'office.

"I'm glad to meet you indeed," states Mr. Edgars. He is wearing tennis shorts, a camouflage bandana, and hiking boots. There is laughter in his eyes and he longs for something in a distance I cannot see. "Well, what do you want to do on the unit?" asks Mr. Edgars. Before I can respond, he quickly stands and hits a tennis ball into the wall. It hits the wall and comes back to him and he continues to hit it. The poor devil doesn't stand a chance. I would save it, but I am scared for my new job. "God, I love that, I just love it. You hit it and it comes back and you get to hit it again. It's damn marvelous. Do you see how it works? Marvelous, is it not?" "Yes, it is marvelous," I agree.

Suddenly he throws the racquet to the floor and sits down. "Tell me, are you a religious man?" he asks as he turns a small ball on his desk upside down, and inside the small ball a snow storm begins. Now I know who played Orson Wells in *Citizen Kane*. If only Hearst were alive. "Do you mean a prophet or holy man, Mr. Edgars?" I blithely inquire, lost in my own wit. "No, no, you seem to have lost the thread of my consciousness here. I mean, do you believe in God? You see, I was once a priest in Belize with a large congregation, but they were lousy tennis players. In fact, they were untrainable, so I left in their good time for a greater flock. Do you play tennis?" asks Mr. Edgars.

"Yes, to a small degree," I reply, "But I was never able to play in Belize. If I had the right priest, I would be at Wimbledon even now." I quickly pull out my racquet and pound a few shots against Mr. Edgars' desk.

PLEASANT GOOD MORNINGS TO YOU

The personnel office is in a basement some thirty stories beneath Dr. Mondriatus' office. There are no elephants in sight. A large sign on the wall states *Support Mental Health*. Underneath it someone has written *Or I'll Kill You*.

Ms. Faragut sits behind her name tag in a large desk that wraps around her and in which she seems intertwined. She has a large pencil in her hand and a small green stuffed bird swings on a perch suspended from her left ear. Nice touch that.

"I'm very secure back here and you are not," she states. "I'm looking for the personnel office," I announce. "I know that," she states. "Go to your right to the first choice point, choose right, and go to the second door."

She is correct concerning the location of the personnel office. The room is painted black with a lot of white signs. A dwarf with a lisp screams, "Who are you and what do you want?" "I'm Dr. Varagon and I want a good and meaningful life, and to fill out my application for employment." The dwarf screams, "That's right, that's too damn right. I've got enough problems running the damn personnel office without having to deal with personnel matters and such. You can have the good and meaningful life, however. Take a seat and I will call you when your number comes up." The dwarf pours a large bag of M&M's onto his desk and begins sorting them according to their colors.

The room is empty save for us and stretches around a corner to unknown climes. I make a mental note to wear a bush jacket if I ever have the misfortune of returning. I pull out a bag of M&M's and begin sorting.

A gong goes off in the distance. "He can see you now," states the dwarf and leads me around the corner to Mr. Obernoff's office. The portal is decorated with designs which appear to be Aztec. I enter a large room bathed in red light. Mr. Obernoff jumps up from his chair and shoos the dwarf out with a flip of his gloved hand. "A more than pleasant good morning to you, young doctor. Please,

please have a chair and be comfortable." Mr. Obernoff sits in the only chair in the room.

"I see everyone who is hired in this place. I am really quite important, although not as important as I used to be at least in the same way you see," states Mr. Obernoff. Then he turns on a movie projector next to his desk and an old newsreel spreads across the wall. "I was in the service as you are probably aware," says Mr. Obernoff. "I was an undertaker, and I know many secrets that you will never know if you do not become an undertaker. There are no dead people here now, or at least there are very few. We used to have a morgue here, but the state decided to remove it as you are aware. That was a pity, sir. I always say "Sir" in just this whining voice because it makes me feel superior in a convoluted sort of way, sir. Do you know you are not even vaguely qualified for your job, although you meet all the requirements. But almost no one is qualified for their job here except me. Do you eat M&M's?" "Yes sir," I state and hand him all my green ones. I love this place, and one day, if I do very well, I will bring the morgue back just for Mr. Obernoff.

MR. BENDER COMES TO CALL

I am acclimatizing myself to the unit. No one else has offered to do so. The hall is long and empty. There is a commode in the patients' lounge with a grobagious palm tree growing from its depths.

In the center of the unit on the north side is a large, heavy metal door with a small window in it. Those desiring admission to the unit must present their heads at the small window unless they have one of the magic keys. Presently there is a large head framed in the small window. Someone is banging on the door. I drag my gnarled leg behind and fumble through the great key chain.

"Jesus, there must be a thousand of the little toads," states the large speaking head. Suddenly Nurse McCroney appears as if by magic, trailing an air of utter confidence. "And what seems to be the problem, Mr. Bunder?" asks Nurse McCroney. Nurse McCroney removes a large hunting knife from her lab coat while stating, "Do not look to the young doctor, he is obviously new here and incompetent for such things." I nod my head wisely.

"You got to help me Nurse McCroney. I'm sick, you old bitch, and surrounded by large green toads wearing Shriners' hats, drinking my rum, and threatening to veto the nurses' union," states Mr. Bunder. "You've been told before that you cannot get away with breaking the rules by sneaking alcohol up here and referring to the nurses as old bitches," states Nurse McCroney. "We deal with sick people here, Mr. Bunder, and there must be organization so that we can dedicate our lives to serving others and retire in thirty years, you silly little man."

"I am a sick person, you old bitch. Does this look well to you?" asks Mr. Bunder as he unzips his fly and pulls out a dead gerbil. "I'll have no more of this one-gerbil-upmanship, Mr. Bunder, as I have sick people to treat," states Nurse McCroney as she summons the guardians of the door who rush Mr. Bunder off to the jungle outside.

The Weeds of God

Nurse McCroney then writes Mr. Bunder's name on a large chart next to the door under the heading, *People We Have Turned Away Today*. Nurse McCroney turns to go, then stops and asks, "You don't believe that stuff about the toads vetoing the union, do you?"

KALEIDOSCOPES AND KNOCKWURST

I seem to be falling down a long corridor with fluffy white clouds. There is a rectangular sofa of friendly sunshine. Mr. Culswamp is speaking. My mind keeps slipping slowly off my shelf of consciousness. It seems so warm where I would be going and immensely pleasing. Mr. Culswamp is speaking.

Mr. Culswamp was born in New York. Apparently we took him prisoner some ten years hence and moved his entire family—yes, all the little Culswamps—to Memphis, Tennessee. "It's like having the very marrow of your intellect sucked dry by a mastodon marrow sucker," states Mr. Culswamp and tips his Panama hat. "There's not one thing here worth knowing except the exits."

Mr. Culswamp looks wistfully into a corner of his mind, possibly the only corner. If you put your ear to the side of Mr. Culswamp's head, you can hear the ocean. "You drink because you are bored?"

"Yes! I am bored by the city, my children, my wife and you. At least when I drink some of it looks more interesting. It gets juxtapositoned and makes a more interesting picture like a fly in a kaleidoscope. You've seen a million of them, but not in that light. My father knew that, and that's why he stayed drunk any time he could find the frigging money. Then I didn't understand. Now I have my own kaleidoscope of my wife's frigging witty sayings, my kid's whining demands, my sister-from-hell's archeological rambling through the Cenozoic era of her endless illnesses, and an ass of a therapist who thinks he's better than me because of the side of the desk he is sitting on. Get the frigging picture? "Some bits of broken glass fall like frozen rainbows on his shoulder. Then Mr. Culswamp's father, Luddy, speaks from the radio on the bookshelf. "Benjamin, you little shit, you are a whining toad. I'm still half glad I killed myself even though you can't get a good knockwurst here to save your soul."

YES, I AM A PSYCHOTHERAPIST

Yes, I am a psychotherapist and I do go out in the noonday sun. I have to because it is very dark where I work. I mine for significance and therapeutic change.

Mr. Geglin, who owns a lot of Mississippi, is talking to me. His father made a lot of money cheating people and Mr. Geglin is half ashamed of his father and half ashamed that he is nowhere near as good at cheating people. His father said things like, "You are a worthless wimp who will never be anything worth being." His father insisted that he play football and be manly. Mr. Geglin never played anything well, although he was able to bleed a lot and whimper. Mr. Geglin's mother, Hermosa, spent all her time bending down to pick up his failures and avoiding the slaps of his father's tongue as she tried to put together a patchwork quilt of minimum emotional damage. Mr. Geglin has never forgiven her for this and other things he has forgotten.

"I don't have a drinking problem. I have a mother problem. She still acts like I'm ten years old." Mr. Geglin kisses his teddy bear and lights another Pall Mall. "I can't take it sometimes, that's all. I just get tired of it. She is everywhere. I find her looking around my mind riding a Harley. If you had her for a mother, you would take a drink or two now and then yourself. I don't deserve this shit. Papa is dead and now I'm the boss, but I don't get to boss anybody. He's dead now and I'm the man of the house. I mean, is this so hard to understand. Forty-five years I did what he said and now I'm supposed to be the boss, but I'm still just listening. I spend most of my time listening to what she has to say."

A large black dog saunters in and calmly urinates on Mr. Geglin's right shoe. The dog looks up at Mr. Geglin and shakes its large fuzzy head vigorously. "She thinks I wanted him dead and that's not true. I loved him more than anything in the world." The dog shakes his head again and leaves. "He loved me. He taught me everything. He was a hard man, but he was fair. He was always fair to me. She remembers things that never happened. She hated him, and I think she was glad when he died. Wait. I know she took care of him, but I think she hated him anyway. I think she liked it when he became an invalid and couldn't feed himself. She liked it. She became the boss. She ran everything. He couldn't even talk or go to the bathroom himself. I think she liked it. It was like a payback for all the things he had done, for all the times he stuck my head in the shit. Now she is him. It's like I've got the whole thing over again and I have to play until I get it right. I'm tired of it. One of these days she will be in that same bed, and I will be there to take her whole life away."

ONCE TO WAR WHILE YOUNG AND VAGABOND

There is an ocean of sound in my ears and I have finished all my charting for this week. It is a beautiful world, and Mr. Hamsung will benefit from my wisdom and my mood. Mr. Hamsung is my 3:30 and a hell of a fellow he is too. He is six feet tall with two seven foot scars across his face and mind. He is on total disability for the plate in his head, a sixteenth century pewter with an Irish coat of arms. This was given to him in Vietnam in the summer of 1967 while he served in the People's Marine Corp. *Semper Fi!*

"I don't drink to forget the war, I drink to forget this shit. How many times have I been in here? Six? Maybe it's seven. What the hell, who keeps count. Body count. I keep body count. That's my thing, you pogue son-of-a-bitch. My own damn thing. What's today? Forget it, it's just another way to count. Do you know there are tribes that have only two numbers - one and more than one. I'm just a one now, but I used to be a more-than-one, but that was long ago and far away." From behind the couch a Hated-Cong peers momentarily, then sinks into the elephant grass. "I can smell them. They smell like stinking fish and wet earth. They followed their mercenary calling and are dead. I was young and vagabond and would have followed Rimbaud to the sands of Iwo Jima. How many Jima's were there and how many now? I am dead too, you unknowing pogue son-of-a-bitch. I am dead too. This is just time left over for us to kill. Each minute is a body count of dead seconds. I am glad to count them with you for you are less of an ass than most. Indeed a sad commentary on my existence that less of an ass is more than I am usually with, even when I am only with myself. What makes me drink?" The passage of the Hated-Cong is marked by the tiniest of whispers through the elephant grass and there is a smell of stinking fish and wet earth. "You will never know. Never. I give only name, rank, and serial number. No more. No more. I will never be that much again. Never. Never be that much again. Where is the connection? Where is the river that ran through us and endlessly beyond and into us again. Where is that damn river? It has stopped. What has dammed it to my soul? Where now does that river run and how can it be found? Sometimes the alcohol seems to make a momentary connection with the river, and I flow again through time and honey colored skies, where I am always young and vagabond. My own sweet love. My own sweet love." The elephant grass whispers sweetly beyond, where the river flows endlessly into each of us and endlessly on. I pull the pin and count to two. The grenade falls into the elephant grass beside our endless river and detonates without sound. Goodbye, old friend. Sleep well, my own sweet love.

HE'S NOT WELL, THAT BOY

Christmas nears and our savior has come. Mr. Ralph Orionto has arrived. He arrives each Christmas about this time. The world believes him to be a chronic, undifferentiated schizophrenic, but each year he crawls to Bethlehem with hopes still high.

This year, the sheriff of the small town near which he lives brought him to the unit. The sheriff claims that, following an emergency call from the home, he arrived at the scene to find Mr. Orionto's mother chasing Mr. Orionto around the house with a large butcher knife. He further indicates that when they came around the next time, Mr. Orionto was chasing his mother with the same butcher knife. He indicates that he intervened at this period because he was getting confused as to who was chasing whom. He proceeded to fire a round from his service revolver into the air as his yelling appeared to be having minimal effect. He further states that Mrs. Orionto continued in her trek around the house. Young Mr. Orionto is said to have stopped, looked up at the heavens, stuck his knife in the side of the house, and proceeded to urinate on a bush growing beside the front door. According to the sheriff, Mr. Orionto then calmly walked up to the officer in a non-threatening manner and stated, "I believe this is a fine day for it. Cogito, ergo sum, and may a persimmon tree blossom from your rectal orifice. Uhum. Uhum. Uhum." Mr. Orionto then opened the backdoor of the sheriff's car, got in, and began mumbling to himself while rocking back and forth. A large, bright star appeared in the heavens and followed the sheriff's car to our facility.

Mr. Orionto's parents have come to the unit to explain why they gave birth to him in a manger and why they believe Herod was a very disagreeable fellow. Mrs. Orionto is wearing a dress with large flowers thrown on it and a hat with a butcher knife for a decoration. She appears slightly older than any stated age and denies hallucinations or delusions while swatting imaginary butterflies with a rolled up copy of the *Wall Street Journal*. Mr. Orionto is wearing a serious expression and denies any stated age. He indicates he plans on killing no one, but that he never plans ahead when he can help it.

"Can you tell me what led up to the incident with the butcher knife?" I ask, while washing my hands in an imaginary basin. "You tell him, Mother," states Mr. Orionto's father while carving his initials in my desk. "Well I think it was the shotgun that set him off." "Shotgun?" I say, before remembering I am never surprised by such trivia. "Yep, it was the shotgun. He got it out of papa's closet and tried to kill us. We were both standing in the hall and the boy just fired the damn thing right at us. I swear I don't think a word was said, he just commenced to firing and that was it." " How could he have fired a shotgun at you in a hall without hitting you?" I stupidly inquire before I can regain composure. "Well it was the air conditioner that saved us. That's what we figure. It must have sucked the pellets right out of the air. It puckered me up a might, I can tell you that. He's not well, that boy and I think he's a damn Lutheran too." Three wise men disguised as psychiatric technicians appear at the door. I fire a shotgun at them, but the pellets are sucked up by the air conditioner.

The Weeds of God

THE CONSULTANT'S CAT

I am a consultant. Weave a circle round me thrice for I will soon feed upon the honeydew and be paid thrice my normal rate because I am a consultant. All experts are strangers. If they know someone as unimportant as you, then they cannot be experts.

I am a consultant at the diagnostic center for the local penal farm every Wednesday from 8:00 am to 10:00 am. The building looks like a treehouse that has fallen to the ground. It is lovingly known as Psychos-East. Many strange and lovely people reside at the center. When I leave at 10:00 am, they cannot be heard if they fall in the wilderness.

Nurse Blithups is standing in the hall, hands on hips and head in the air as if catching the scent of some small prey in the distance. He is six feet tall with tattoos and scars. His head is shaved and there is mild psychomotor agitation present. His last job was at a chicken processing plant where he was fired for brutality.

"I say Clidders is not stabilized by his medication and should stay put, Doc. That's how I see it and I'm here every day," states Nurse Blithups as he maintains unflinching eye contact, wrestling my right cornea to the mat for a three point pin. "I say that using that as an opening statement to everyone you meet will get you in this place sooner or later, and that's how I see it and I'm here every Wednesday." Heavens, I am such the playful lad.

"Joke if you want to, Doc, but he's still crazy." I'm destroyed. The logic is overpowering. "Mr. Clidders is afflicted with Huntingtons Chorea besides his relatively stabilized paranoid schizophrenia. Who do you think he will harm on the outside. Is he going to specialize in quadriplegics? He couldn't catch a snail and he can no longer talk or write well enough to rob a lemonade stand." I pull out a large flashlight and look into Nurse Blithup's left ear while humming the Captain Bogey march.

"He's still seeing the cat. He is actively hallucinating," states Nurse

Blithup while bringing down the gavel on my head. Mr. Clidders has been saying a large gray cat comes to sleep on his chest each night since he arrived. Since being told he cannot go home if he is actively hallucinating, he has not mentioned the problem. It's raining on Mr. Clidders' parade. Dr. Isenloaf refuses parole to anyone with active hallucinations. When asked why, he always states, "It's a rule." Heavens, it just makes the whole thing worthwhile. Dr. Isenloaf is the Director of Psychiatric Services and even a bigger expert than me because he is never here. I have only talked to him on the phone and no one has ever seen him. Now there is an expert indeed. Who are mere mortals to question the Master of Psychic Vivisection?

"Come on back and ask him yourself," states Nurse Blithup and heads off canter levered to the East. The massive steel door opens to "their world". It is dark and damp and there are bats hanging from the ceiling in small chains. The ward is a rectangle that goes endlessly into the distance. Mr. Clidders is laying on the top bunk in bed number twelve. He lays motionless staring at the ceiling. On his chest sits a large gray cat. The cat's tail flicks back and forth, back and forth across Mr. Clidders' face. The cat looks at us contemptuously and returns to washing its paws as its tail flicks back and forth, back and forth across Mr. Clidders' face. "Jesus," states Nurse Blithup, "there is a damn cat." "I don't see him either," states Mr. Clidders and continues to stare at the ceiling. Dr. Freud sits up on his bottom bunk, and peeks up at Mr. Glidders. "I don't see him either," states Dr. Freud as he rips pages from *Symbols in Transformation*.

FORTY-ONE AND DONE

I am in one of the endless corridors of the unit headed for the relative safety of my office. Black fog fills the hall to about waist height. The sound of albatross wings can be heard in the distance. A boat filled with derelicts makes its way against the morning tide. Star shells light the hall, but the boat hugs the side of the hall refusing to recognize even the possibility of rescue.

Mrs. Huddle floats into my office on a piece of driftwood. Mrs. Huddle has been married for eight years to Ragnor the Abysmal. "We were happy once," states Mrs. Huddle and I fear she means this to be true.

The Huddles have been unhappy a long, long time. Mrs. Huddle's child died two days after she was born. Mrs. Huddle is unable to have any more children. Mrs. Huddle drinks a fifth of bourbon every day and gives birth to sadness all forlorn.

"He never hit me before I started drinking," states Mrs. Huddle. There is a large clock on Mrs. Huddle's wall with fifty second hands all moving to a different concept of time. Only Mrs. Huddle knows how they should be aligned. Every morning about half-past three she sets the hands with loving care.

"I don't love him. You know that by now, but you don't know the fear of leaving, of starting again. Who would want me now? It takes so long to build a new relationship, a relationship that is something of meaning. I always wanted a special kind of relationship. I want to be happy, but I'm not sure what is to be happy. I know you think I should leave, but I don't have any place to leave to. Forty-one years old is too old to get back into the market place. It's not that bad where I am when you think of the alternatives. I'm so used to it now. It's not so bad, really," says Mrs. Huddle.

WE ARE CLINICIANS, ONE AND ALL

It is 4 o'clock and the day is done. All the patients are enjoying maximum hospital benefits and looking forward to another of our sumptuous meals prepared by members of the Georgia chain-gang. I seek salvation in small places.

The walk to the bar in the basement of a nearby high-rise apartment leads me past the remains of an ancient mound-building culture, the noble Octawhapahos. Their mounds rise in sensuous curves on the grounds of my beloved state hospital. I feel a stirring connection with these beings who left a signpost in time. Now winos graze on brown paper bags where their moccasined feet once tread. Longfellow is buried here with only a wisp of a poem to mark his passing.

The bar is lovely, dark and deep. There is a maze of passage ways that isolates each island of revelers and passing acquaintances. Just lovely. The waiter appears carrying a stone ax and brooding over the large Magdalenian Venus he is carving in the bar. "Rum and coke?" He has already brought it with him and I know clinically that I could destroy his delicate psyche if I refuse. "Know that you have won the love of a prince," and I graciously accept.

Around the table sit five grandmasters of psychic vivisection. Dr. Littelpon states, "I am going to kill that bitch one of these days." All of us nod our heads in solemn agreement for this obviously logical clinical decision. Virtually all of us who have had the horror of meeting Mrs. Littlepon would cheerfully kill her. My first meeting with her was in this bar. Dr. Littelpon was sitting in his usual chair with his back to the door. In walked the lovely Mrs. Littelpon. I watched as her vision acclimatized to the darkness. Then she set forth towards her husband, stopping momentarily to pluck a beer bottle out of the hand of a nearby patron. Without saying a word, she struck Dr. Litlepon a fine blow to the left temple that dropped him off the chair like a felled ox. She turned to the group and stated, "You silly bunch of little boys." All of us nodded agreement and, satisfied, she headed out the door. After a short sojourn in the emergency room and five stitches, Dr. Littelpon was once again ready for battle. He had no lasting aftereffects except from time to time he would blurt out "351 South Dunlap" for no apparent reason. We later discovered this was the address of the church in which they were married.

The latest incident is much more fascinating and demonstrates a cunning that can only be described as brilliant. Dr. and Mrs. Littelpon were having one of their scheduled evening arguments with accompanying physical attacks, when Mrs. Littlepon suddenly stated, "Your right, John, I have been a total bitch. Please forgive me, my love." She then begged Dr. Littelpon to prepare himself for a sexual experience that would leave him wreathing in the ecstasy he deserved. Momentarily stunned, he stated, "351 South Dunlap", and rushed off to undress. Having undressed, he waited for the beloved Mrs. Littelpon, He heard the front door open, felt a blast of the cold December night, and then detected the sound of metal hitting concrete. He rushed out of the bedroom to find his wife throwing more of his gun collection out the front door into the snow. After pausing to slap the lovely Mrs. Littelpon one good blow to the head, he rushed into the night to retrieve his guns. Mrs. Littelpon then closed and locked the front door behind him. When the police arrived, they found themselves facing a large nude man holding two Purddy shotguns and beating on the front door of the house. He was surrounded by a virtual arsenal of weapons, and was repeating "351 South Dunlap" over and over again. Needless to say they were not interested in any explanations. After cuffing him and placing him in the squad car, they asked the lovely Mrs. Littelpon if she knew the man who claimed to be her husband. She stated that she had never seen him before he appeared on the lawn with enough weapons to start a small war. She further stated that her husband was a psychiatrist and this could well be one of his violent patients, and that they should possibly take him to the state facility for the insane. They did.

Today Dr. Littelpon is a wiser man and never sits with his back to the door in any bar. He also has a change of clothes in his car and a complete set of identification. Dr. Littelpon's mother considers Mrs. Littelpon to be a wonderful person with an impish since of humor. Dr. Littelpon's mother is just as lovely as his wife, but he has never noticed this reality. We are clinicians, one and all.

THREE CHEETAHS AND A BABY GAZELLE

My 2 o'clock is here, Mr. Meminon of Ludlow Shire. He brings his own darkness with him. It oozes into the room and snuggles into every available corner. "Come quick, Bwana, witch doctor makeum ju-ju." Herds of elephant graze in the plain and Mount Kilimanjaro rises to the clear blue sky unconcerned with Mr. Meminon and his small problems.

Mr. Meminon is a white male appearing his stated age. He is seriously depressed and suicidal ideation is present. His WAIS IQ is 162 and he is very solemn about his twenty-five years of life. The world would appear to be his for the asking. He has had three one man shows at local art galleries, and his paintings are selling to the rich and famous. He smokes Lucky Strikes and has a gold Dupont lighter given to him by a very beautiful woman who visits him with joyous regularity. "Come quick, Bwana, witch doctor makeum ju-ju."

"It is all red in tooth and claw, good doctor. Is it not? Each second brings more pain. Four million years of evolution and we eat our fellow beings. Do you know what kosher is, good doctor? We slit their throats so they cannot frighten us with their suffering. We do not wish to hear what we do. If they make no noise, we can pretend we make no pain. We are vile brutes. Each day millions are killed that we may eat at McDonald's. Sad, is it not? Each steak is part of some poor being we have butchered and packaged for consumption. It frightens me. I am frightened by the beast who lives inside my mind. I am frightened by my own rage, and the joy of harming your fellow beings. Once when I was a boy I saw God. I was a carry-out boy at Kroger. I was sixteen years old and I do not know how old God was then. He carried a can of Spam in a hand splotched with time. He was old, very old and shabby. His clothes belonged to many people that had gone before and he smelled of time and its refuse. His eyes were yellow and expected betrayal and humiliation. The checker looked at him with the contempt of youth for its own tomorrows and snapped his finger for God to attend to the speed of our age. God fumbled through His many empty pockets for the change borrowed from the streets and crawled into the darkness of another day. I love you, God, and I am so sad. I am so sad, I would like to kill the smirking little ass and lay him at Your feet. I am so sad that this is all there is of life even when there is more." Mr. Meminon lights another Lucky Strike and stares out the window at a vast herd of gazelles passing swiftly in the distance. "Can it be this is the sum of all things? I think so. I think so. Yesterday or the yesterday before, I saw the play of life. I saw all of it in one small scene. There were three cheetahs and a baby gazelle. There was a mother cheetah and two cubs. The mother lay serenely contemplating the beauty of a bountiful day while her two children played around her. They played with a baby gazelle their mother had found for them. The baby gazelle frolicked between the two cubs as they clubbed her with their small paws. Was she so happy to play with her new companions that she forgot her mother standing forlorn in the distance unable to prevent the carnage so soon to come? The play seemed to go on endlessly. The baby gazelle was all the beautiful, gentle things you have ever seen. Then the play ended and the baby was only a red rag ripped apart by tooth and claw. There is no blame here. That is the great tragedy. That has always been the great tragedy of the whole damn thing. When I take the heroin, that sweet white goddess, I sometimes think I see a way to climb to the rim of this madness and pull myself out. It fades as the drug fades, and I must start again." "Come Kimo Sebe, we ride like wind."

AM I MAKING MYSELF UNDERSTOOD?

The wind is whistling through the willows. In the corner of the room a large bullfrog sits on a lily pad and whistles with the willows. This is an enchanted land indeed.

Today the hated paperwork must be done. There are five hundred charts to make notes in and two clinical staff meetings. No one gets to see patients because we are too busy documenting that we saw patients. Now I have to see Mr. Cromwhit's wife that she may sign all the papers that give us permission to do all the things we may do to her husband.

Mr. Cromwhit is a connoisseur of paregoric. Actually he is a connoisseur of codeine, but he has to drink a lot of paregoric to get it. Pharmacies can presently dispense one bottle of paregoric with codeine without a prescription which means he must make the rounds of numerous pharmacies to get enough to get the job done. Maybe it's the paregoric and the wonderful process involved that he really likes. He has six type written sheets with schedules of different pharmacies he visits to obtain the massive number of paregoric bottles he needs to feed his habit. Amazingly enough, he is a well known contractor who finishes his jobs on time. Of course he has fallen off more roofs than a man could shake a stick at, but it has apparently had little serious effect. Mr. Cromwhit is very sad that the state is passing a law forbidding his beloved paregoric with codeine from being sold without a prescription. Another damn middle man to deal with and once again the puritan swine are taking away all our fun.

Mrs. Cromwhit has arrived one hour early. Sorry, cannot attend staffing due to clinical necessities. God bless you Mrs. Cromwhit. Mrs. Cromwhit is six feet tall and weighs in at about two hundred and fifty pounds. There are grizzly bears that would leave an elk kill if Mrs. Cromwhit appeared on the scene. She fills up the office like a size fourteen foot in a size four slipper. She is pleasant and signs all of the documents without asking any of the questions I can't answer. "Can I ask you some questions, doctor?" I knew it, I

The Weeds of God

knew it was too good to be true. "It's about my husband." God bless you, Mrs. Cromwhit.

"It's about his sexual performance. Well, it's about his lack of sexual performance really. We haven't had sex in eight months. It was October 8th at 4:00 pm. That's a long time, a long time. Do you see what I'm asking?" "Of course Mrs. Cromwhit, I understand completely," said in my most reassuring voice. Mrs. Cromwhit slowly stands up. She is wearing a flowered dress. Suddenly she reaches down and pulls the hem of her dress up to her chin, and states, "am I making myself understood?" She is nude except for a garter belt, a garter belt that could easily pull a four ton truck out of a quagmire. There is more flesh here than Rubens saw in a lifetime. Jesus H. Christ. There is a knock at the door. Mrs. Cromwhit's dress falls like the curtain at the Metropolitan Opera. Nurse Minder sticks her head in, "Dr. Littelpon says your patients need to be staffed." "Of course, of course, Mrs. Minder. Mrs. Cromwhit has finished all her paper work." Never, never avoid staffing and always take plenty of paregoric with codeine if you want to survive in this troubled world.

I BICK YOU

Mr. Lessmore stairs at the three tattoos on his left arm. They read *Born to Lose* in large red script, once in English, once in Latin and once in Greek. He picks at them from time to time and gazes into a distance I cannot see. "Do you know what the word verbatim means?" I quickly ruffle through the pages of my verbatim memory and cleverly respond, "What does it mean, Mr. Lessmore?"

"Nothing really, nothing can be word for word. There are words not intended and words not said and words said too often to be real and words said so often they go unnoticed, but no words are said word for word. Do you believe in the power of the word? Are words always the beginning and the end? I **bick** you." I am lost, Mr. Lessmore. What are you? What has caused the sudden and rapid deterioration of your being? We have diagnosed you as schizophrenic, but what the hell are you really and what do I do to help? For twenty-eight years you led the most normal of lives. You have one wife, two children, two cars and two degrees from Yale. You make a good living and attend church every Sunday. Then most suddenly, four months ago, you become psychotic. There is no history of mental illness in your family. There have been no major traumas in your life during the past six years. What are you, Mr. Lessmore? Where have you gone and why, or what has come to you and why? Has it become too much or too little that you should decide to leave?

Four months ago on Friday, Mr. Lessmore walked into the center of main street at 12:00 am. He was nude and carried a grocery sack. He pulled six cantaloupes out of the sack and arranged them in a large circle. He then proceeded to defecate in the middle of the circle of cantaloupes. After cleaning himself with a tie ripped from the neck of a bystander, he stood and said, "Well, that about does it." He then held two hands up toward the sun stating, " Who here can deny that Jupiter has a diameter of 88, 640 miles, give or take a cubit or two? Can you believe that such a mass has no effect on your daily lives? I think not, my fellow travelers. I think not indeed. Do the words Fomahalut, Betelgeuse, Capella and Sirius mean nothing to you?" A crowd had encircled Mr. Lessmore. One large man with a brown paper bag yelled, "Frigging Al Capone and Spiro been screwing us as long as I can remember." At which point, he fell forward into the magic circle with a thud to mark his passing. Mr. Lessmore then attacked his fallen acolyte, but was pulled away from this task by a large policeman unaware of the diameter of Jupiter. Two hours later, Mr. Lessmore arrived at our sacred grove.

Mr. Lessmore's mother came to see me yesterday. The social history completed by his mother reads like a script from *Father Knows Best*. You cannot find enough trauma to fill a thimble. Mr. Lessmore's mother is a small women with quick, precise gestures. She arranged all the objects on my desk in neat, orderly rows and then went to work on my collection of inconsequential sayings getting to alphabetical listing "u" before stopping to tell me of a prize she would share. "It's the self-abuse. When he was a child, he used to abuse himself two or three times a day. I caught him at it on many an occasion and whipped him good. He had all manner of pornographic magazines too. That's what got him in this fix. It's stopped up his mind." I thank Mr. Lessmore's mother, slip a pornographic magazine into her purse, and send her on her way to organize an unsuspecting world.

Is this it? Did the maze of obsessive-compulsive magic that held the dark powers break? Could you have sustained such a superhuman effort over twenty-eight years without any suggestion of strain? Do you attempt to heal the breach by seeking the help of the old gods who held each moment of the day in their capable hands? What an agony you must have known with each second holding the infinite possibility that all the world would be unraveled. Now once again you can sleep, having summoned the very marrow of organized certainty to your side. Each blade of grass and the wind that touches it are part of an infinite pattern that unfolds exactly in its appointed place. I need this certainty too, Mr. Lessmore. I cannot reach you. I do not understand. We have given you our magic potions from the mistletoe, and now we watch for the rebirth of the boring, solid, perfectly rational Mr. Lessmore. This morning I went to the grove and sang the sun into its path across the sky. I sat beneath the great oak waiting for the touch of knowledge that would give you unto me, but only a clock came ticking to summon me from thought. I too am lost, Mr. Lessmore, and I **bick** you.

NYX NOX NYX

"Nyx nox nyx and a bowl of bicks," sings Mr. Lessmore as he dances nude in the hall. Not your average bear, Mr. Lessmore. He is certainly adding a bit of excitement to the unit. I must look at the recreational therapy schedule and see if the lovely Ms. Bodryright has added something new. "Special duty, Three East. Special duty, Three East." The intercom will soon summon the guardians of order from their dens. "Uhum, uhum, that's me. I'm special duty, lots of special duty. Nyx nox nyx and a bowl of bicks. Special duty get your kicks. I'm here and here and everywhere, nyx nox nyx." Head nurse Lilly "Bitch" Holstein stands at the unit door. She is wearing a Viking helmet and carrying a large spear. She is about to sing. I love this place.

Mr. Lessmore is soon cocooned and suspended in time in a small, dark room. Nurse Holstein is breathing fire from her nostrils and heading in my direction. I retreat toward the men's restroom to hide. I am such a brave lad. "He wouldn't be doing that if he was appropriately medicated," roars Nurse Holstein as she enters the men's room, throws back her cape and looks to the heavens. "Who wrote *Kill Brunehilde* on the men's bathroom wall? I don't think you are so damn witty. And no matter what the others think, I think you are an incompetent ass."

"Actually, I think the others think I am a witty, incompetent ass. And what are you doing in the men's restroom, and what makes you think Brunehilde refers to you, and why can't you sing a decent aria?" I have almost reached the unit door, my Parthian arrows flung.

"I'm going to suggest electric shock therapy to Dr. Littlepon," sings Nurse Brunehilde to the heavens. "Well, I think I can back you up on that brilliant clinical decision. Dr. Littlepon could use a few volts and I might add, you could use a few volts yourself. There is no possibility it could damage your delicate psyche and there is always the chance that it could improve your singing voice." Jesus, I am almost out of ammo and the bitch is gaining on me.

New tactic. "Wait, Nurse Holstein. I apologize for speaking to you in such a manner. There is something about the way you present yourself that seems to stir all the more puckish elements in my personality. I promise in the future to try to better understand your point of view and refrain from any stupid remarks. Can you accept my apology?"

Nurse Holstein is momentarily staggered. "Well I, I mean I guess sometimes . . . "

"Thank you, Nurse Holstein." Now I am away, speeding down the hall. Now that's clinical magic, you bitch, and nyx nox nyx.

A PRETTY PLACE

Ms. Saddenlis is fondling the bandages on her wrists. Two weeks ago her mother found her in the bathtub with a sea of red foam gurgling around her. "Her head was to the side and she was smiling. She wasn't even conscious and she was smiling like she had seen something nice." I wonder what she saw sitting in a spreading pool of herself on a Saturday night in Memphis, Tennessee. I wonder what she saw, this so lovely child.

Ms. Saddenlis is a sixteen year old white female looking older than her stated age. She is incredibly beautiful with long blond hair and sad green eyes that seem never to focus. There is great pleasure in looking at her. She seems so soft and vulnerable. You feel like holding her and telling her all will be well. There is another part still in my mind mixed in with this kindness of purpose. I lust for her in dark corners of quiet places and I want her to admire me. I wish this were not there, but I know it sits waiting. Will I speak to be admired and make her indebted to the god of psychic vivisection that she may fall under the foolish spell I would weave? I must concentrate on what is best for her and eliminate the me from the spell I will weave.

Her father has beaten her. He has not beaten her with his fists, but with words. Each day she was struck over and over again. She was told how special she was and how perfect she must be to deserve to be special. As she grew older the demands for perfection increased until the great disaster occurred. Boys begin to look at her with the same lust I feel. "You must keep yourself perfect and fight the vileness of the devil within you," said her father as he fought the vileness of the devils within him. "You must keep yourself pure or suffer the fate of the damned. Stay away from them because they only want one thing. They are defilers, defilers and beasts." Her mother hid in the yard planting flowers and in the kitchen with recipes that had always worked before.

But Angus cannot be stopped by bolts and chains of words or steel. He came to this fair maiden as he comes to all. She fell from grace in the back seat of his car in a moment that seemed quite magical at the time.

But Angus must tell of his deeds or lose the splendor he holds over the gods who only plod through their appointed rounds. He told and others told in their turn to hold momentarily the stage of light. And she heard. She heard and fell again. What she had found of a magic quite pure became a vile, darkening thing spreading in her mind. And then her father heard and the darkening thing filled all the world.

"It was such a pretty place. It was all light, light within spreading, deepening light. I saw it quite clearly. It was such a pretty place. It is where I want to be."

EVEN NOTHING CANNOT LAST FOREVER

Mr. Godnit sits on the edge of his chair and peers into his shoe. It is a Florshiem size nine and a half in burgundy. His eyes rove the inside contours of the shoe as if watching the movement of some small beast. I wish to look too, or pull my own shoe off and have a squint, but I refrain. "Have any idea what it means?" asks Mr. Godnit. I refrain from responding, but look attentive.

"Why do so many beautiful things die? What are we waiting for? Why do we not revolt and kill this all too brutal god? Look at the horror that surrounds you. We are Shiva. We are the evil that men do. I wish no part of it. There are so many people I would like to kill, but I am a coward. I am afraid of killing them and I am afraid of killing myself. My hate is so real I can feel it falling out of me into the room. I have some for you. I have some for everyone. Why can I not be brave enough to either kill myself or the rest of you? It's God's joke on all of us. We are each other's joke, every damned one of us." Mr. Godnit pulls out a picture of his daughter and stares deep into it. She is four years old and has Down's syndrome and spinal bifida. Mr. Godnit puts the picture of his daughter into his shoe. "I'm Buster Brown, look for me in there too," states Mr. Godnit. His daughter died five weeks ago.

"What do you live for? Do you really care what I feel? I don't care what you feel. In a way I hate you. I would kill you to save a single hair on my child's head. Disgusting. Disgusting. I am all the things I hate. I hear too many voices and too many thoughts. I feel like turning them all off. I could not help her. Maybe no one can really help anyone. You are not helping me, you are just passing time for your money. I wish my wife was dead. She could not help either and now she tells me it was God's will. Even nothing cannot last forever, and all of this is now nothing. I hate your God. It will never end, this hate, and now it is all I have. I hate my wife. I like watching her and knowing that I hate her and her bland, sanctimonious shit. I wish to live with her forever and follow her with my hate. No, I wish to lead her with my hate like a seeing eye dog before its master's step. She is a statement by God of His ridiculousness."

Mr. Godnit sits on the edge of his chair with his hand inside his shoe holding his lost child's picture. He rocks back and forth. The wind blows sand across the floor of tiles and, in the distance, the Nile forms a dark ribbon of life. There is single falcon held aloft on a platform of air that is stretched far above the desert in a blue river of time. Even nothing cannot last forever.

AIN'T NO BIG THING

A light rain is falling. It whispers against my window. Mr. Carsenullers has been medicated and it is not raining where he lives. Mr. Carsenullers is wearing a T-shirt with the words *Knows the Seldon Plan*. He is looking at his left hand. He turns it over and examines the other side. Very interesting.

He used to be very interesting. He used to be very manic. Four Sundays hence, when he was a prince among men, he drove a tractor with a harrow up on the mayor's front lawn and proceeded to prepare the entire area for planting. His accomplishment was not looked upon with favor by the mayor, a man with all the personality of a ruptured racquet ball but with none of the panache. The mayor had Mr. Carsenullers arrested. Mr. Carsenullers denied culpability, indicating that the mayor had asked him to plant a cotton crop for him, and he was simply lending the helping hand.

A year ago he was arrested at the bank when he tried to sell them on the idea of using a new bill that he had invented. On one side it was a twenty and on the other it was a ten. Mr. Carsenullers pointed out that it was the only bill that could make change for itself. The bank president did not see the obvious benefit and had him locked up. All charges were dismissed by a judge who had a sense of humor.

Two years ago he painted a sign on the Republican presidential campaign headquarters reading, *Nixon Died for Your Sins and So Should Bush*. He was charged with defacing private property, but when his stated defense was that nothing could further deface such a concept, all charges were dropped.

He is now on a stabilizing regimen of lithium, because Dr. Nickrick has found out that Mr. Carsenullers is a manic-depressive. Mr. Carsenullers is very stable. He is oriented to time, place and person and could easily be mayor of our fair city. There is presently a manifest lack of poetry in Mr. Carsenullers. Where lithium goes, poetry leaves. He is now closely examining a fingernail on his right index finger. I may take a look at it myself if things continue in this vein.

Tonight I will free Mr. Carsenullers. I will open his cage and help him fly away. Yesterday I called his mother who lives in Oxford, Mississippi. I disguised my voice as that of our beloved leader, Dr. Nickrick. First, I put a handkerchief over the phone, then I hit myself with a ballpeen hammer, and the impersonation was virtually perfect. I told her that her son would be leaving on a bus for her lovely city and that he was fine as long as he stayed away from lithium. I told her it would be best if he took a little vacation from Memphis, maybe two or three years.

Oxford is a fine place for Mr. Carsenullers. They appreciate the Mr. Carsenullers of the world in Oxford. The world needs a little plowing from time to time.

MRS. DENDRITUS

Mrs. Dendritus sits rigidly in the chair across from my desk. She is dressed in a discarded rainbow she found in a discarded garbage can. "I can't take much more of this foolishness," she states.

I am tempted to tell her just how much foolishness you can take if you put your mind to it, but I'm pretty sure this would not be therapeutic. "This whole place has industrial strength negative vibes," she says while holding a wooden cross in my direction. This is something with which I can readily agree.

"My father raped me on my thirteenth birthday . . . kind of a birthday present I guess," said while she stares at the wooden cross in her lap. "I told my mother and she slapped me . . . kind of a birthday present I guess."

"I still loved him, that's what's so strange. I can't remember not loving him. I hated my mother then and I hate her now. I wish she had died rather than him. Do you know why he died?" I make no reply because I'm the therapist.

"He died because I poisoned him. I slept with him in his mind and left a poison. I don't think I meant to, but maybe I did. He never slept with my sister," she says with a sly smile and straightens her dress.

YESTERDAY'S SUBMARINE

The water is calm. The world is all blue water as far as the eye can see. "Prepare to surface. Battle stations surface." I turn my hat back to front and clamp the periscope to my eye.

It has been a long war. We have only two torpedoes left, and no hot sauce for the beans. I am thinking of the lovely Caroline Stiffwhomper, a tall blond with the brains of a train whistle. I also remember our brothers who sleep beneath the waves.

There is a knock at the door. It will be Mr. Sllystaller for his two o'clock session. I let the boat sink slowly beneath the waves and remove my captain's hat. "It smells like saltwater in here," says Mr. Sllystaller. He has been doing cocaine for five years since he found out it could make life momentarily interesting for him. He tests out at a 156 IQ on the WAIS and has his own investment firm.

"Did you know Freud did coke?" asks Mr. Sllystaller as he moves his chair out of a puddle of salt water. He proceeds to tell me many things about Dr. Freud. "I don't treat Dr Freud anymore, Mr. Sllystaller. Let's get back to you." "It is me," says Mr. Sllystaller. "Then can you tell me your real relationship with Dr. Jung and your latest concepts concerning the libido?" I ask mind awhirl with the possibility of new discoveries.

"It is me because, like Freud, like everybody, all my behavior is determined by my past learning and genetic inheritance to which I am enslaved, "says Mr. Sllystaller while telling Chief Warrant Officer Paulus to level the boat at sixty-nine feet. "It is not that I have no choice, it is that I have no freedom to have chosen those choices leading to the inevitability of the present choice in each becoming instant of time." The boat levels off at sixty-nine feet.

"It was inevitable that you would be addicted to cocaine?" I ask. "I am not addicted to cocaine," states Mr. Sllystaller, "I use cocaine. Yes, it was inevitable that I would use cocaine. It was inevitable that I would find the feeling of rushing joy worth the purchase price in terms of money and danger. It was inevitable that I would find the danger of purchase exhilarating. All this was inevitable, but I am not addicted," states Mr. Sllystaller while searching the horizon through the periscope for new victims.

"You are, in a sense, addicted to your past learning experiences and your genetic inheritance?" I say for no apparent reason. "You are, in a sense, playing word games," says Mr. Sllystaller as a new victim appears on the horizon. " We are in a sense playing word games," I state while ordering the crew to use a zig-zag course to avoid torpedoes.

STERILE GHOSTS

The halls are sterile. The whole damn place is sterile. The sterile ghosts of thousands of patients nod as I pass them in the hall.

I will see Mr. Klinsky in thirty minutes. Soon he will be another sterile ghost inhabiting our halls. I know this because Dr. Blatt told me so in staffing after Mr. Klinsky told him he was an obnoxious son-of-a-bitch in front of the head nurse.

Nurse Carla Metzenhiem – just call me Carl – first suggested decapitating patient Klinsky, but a careful review of state regulations revealed we were over our decapitation limit for the season. Dr. Blatt retired to his office where he studied his degrees and then became comatose for two hours. Nurse Carl disturbed his revery to suggest an industrial strength enema was called for, but Dr. Blatt refused with many thanks, not realizing she was referring to Mr. Klinsky. Mr. Klinsky, not realizing his good fortune, continued to roam the halls searching for other authority figures to disembowel.

Soon he will come striding into my office to discuss recent kills and why he has no problems and has learned to stop fighting his good fortune and simply live it. At some time during the session he will discuss his past martyrdom and testify to the fact that no one pushes him around anymore.

"Good morning Mr. Klinsky," and I shake his hand as if we hadn't been seeing each other three times a week for the last month. Otherwise, Mr. Klinsky looks very sad and says, "You don't have the manners to shake hands with an old man?"

"I talked to my daughter today, "states Mr. Klinsky. "She's trying to put me on a guilt trip, but I don't do that shit anymore. Her mother is her problem, not mine. The bitch got all my money, my house and my damn car. Then my sweet daughter goes to live with her, so let her make her own bed. I don't give a damn. Both of them are as exciting as an empty can of pinto beans." Mr. Klinsky pauses for breath and lights another cigarette.

"They have been boring me for the past fifteen years. Now I'm not guilty about admitting it. I can't stand either of them. Every day I can remember was a cacophony of 'give-me's' and 'I want's' from those bitches. Boring! Boring! Well now I want, I want to be excited by life again. They gave me so much boring, I can't remember what exciting is like. They plastered me over with boring. The bitch left me for a lawyer. Jesus H. Christ, a lawyer and he's as boring as they are for God's sake. I feel like killing somebody." And he looks at me.

I wonder if it would be therapeutic to tell him I find the whole thing boring too. No. I'll just go back in my mind where I hide from Mr. Klinsky and wait for him to reach maximum hospital benefits.

THE EGYPTIANS

There is someone screaming in room 309. His screams wander down the halls knocking on every useless door. Help! Help! The screams stop for a moment and the corridors breathe a sigh of relief.

They start again with a vengeance. Room 309 is a detox room and someone is screaming that we may give unto him his opiate alkaloids so he may dine on something other than pain unending. We know what is best. Heroin ruins your veins and constipates you, you foolish lad.

The nurses are reasoning with him. "It will all be over soon and you can start a new life," states Nurse Akbar the Petulant. "Dr. Mondriatus has even decided not to remove your leg," she adds while driving around his bed in a golf-cart. He is strapped to the bed in six point restraints because we are trying to teach him as many points as we can in the midst of his pain. This is an excellent time for learning.

The patient is being unreasonable. He continues to scream and whine, reminding us of our pitiful humanity. Everyone is very embarrassed and tries to appear professional and detached. Suddenly everyone is very, very busy with other activities as far away from room 309 as possible.

Room 309 contains a permanent scream from all the poor souls who have gone before. You can see it peeking out of the room when it has no company, like a small kitten in a cage with its paw extended through the wire. Will no one help? Will no one come?

The screams stop. The patient in room 309 yells, "The Egyptians were able to train baboons to serve their dining tables. Can we expect less of nurses and physicians?"

Nurse Akbar the Petulant asks Dr. Mondriatus, "Is that true?" "I'm not sure," answers Dr. Mondriatus, "but I've certainly had my suspicions about the waitresses in the cafeteria." The screams begin again and Dr. Mondriatus and Nurse Akbar the Petulant head for the cafeteria.

YESTERDAY'S LOVE

Mr. James is one of the most interesting people in the world. He is twenty-five years old and appears younger than his stated age. He is actively hallucinating (visual and auditory) and delusional thought is present. He manifests ideas of reference, and severe paranoid ideation is present. He is a poly-drug abuser including, but not necessarily limited to, heroin, cocaine, methamphetamine, hallucinogens and various combinations. He denies hallucinations, but he is delusional on this point. Two days ago both of us talked with Pope Urban VI, whom he insisted on referring to as Prigy.

Mr. James has been hospitalized on numerous occasions. He knows more therapeutic techniques than your average bear, and he is frequently saddened by the inadequacies of those who attempt to treat him. With this I can wholeheartedly agree.

"I had sex with my sister," states Mr. James. "I had sex with my sister since I was fourteen years of age. Many great men had sex with their sisters. Caligula had sex with his sister and he was a great man. Did he not make a horse a senator, thus in one fell swoop forever limiting the equestrian order? Was he not a ligula, and am I not a ligula too, but I never had sex with his sister. I'm guilty like a dog. I am the dog of hell and my father is the progenitor of hell and all its dogs. I have seen a room with a million doors, and each leads to hell and from hell because the journey is the same. You tell me it is my perception that makes me guilty. Then your perception of my perception makes you guilty too. I have more word games, and you are not half the sly fox you pretend although you are somewhat superior to the others in your quaint way."

Mr. James is tearing up a sheet of paper. The tears are very uniform. He places each small piece on my desk in an intricate mandala of madness. He seems to know where each piece must go. There are unseen marks upon the desk that guide him to each placement.

"She stopped when I was eighteen and said, 'no more.' I do not know why she stopped for all she would say was, 'it was time.' I have asked her many times since and always her answer is the same. An old gray cat each day at three appears like magic by the big elm tree . . . it is a construction. They construct my madness out of their words. Filaments of evil spun fine around me and discarded bits and pieces of some truth. You too are one of these and can no more escape your fate than I." I begin to tear small pieces from Mr. James' paper and we construct the mandala as one.

MR. CLAPO'S ARGUMENT

I have created, at Dr. Mondriatus' request, a federal grant that sucks great wads of money into our darkened tunnel. It is to provide services for narcotics addicts that they may be made well and bore the world with their heartfelt thanks for our endeavors. The federal government demands that matching money be provided by the city government, so that the guilt of such actions can be shared.

I have come to the city council to plead my case. I am nervous in an unknowing kind of way.

Mr. Lemme, the chairman of the city council, says that his grandfather, Papa Lemme, invented graft just after he developed the cholera virus. Many people say that Mr. Lemme is a braggart and a Republican, but these are hard accusations to prove in our neighborhood.

Our grant is twenty-second on the agenda. It comes after a "deceleration of gratitude to the Pochadope Indians for selling Memphis to white men for a ridiculous number of beads and promptly dying of cholera."

To open the meeting, Reverend Steinthud reads fifty pages of a benediction praising every aspect of American society, and giving Jesus credit for inventing convertibles. Next, Mr. Lemme asks if anyone has read the minutes of last week's meeting, and a fist fight ensues between members who think this refers specifically to the council board and those believing it refers to minutes of any meeting held last week.

The first item on the agenda is the condemnation of a building. Mr. Plum with the city engineers states, "Yep, it's still right putrid and an eye sore for damn sure." Then the owner, Mr. Clapo, states, "I'm about getting around to fixing her up, and if you'll be kind enough to give me another thirty days, I'll have her done." Mr. Letts, who has been on the council two hundred years asks, "Haven't we given you twenty extensions already?"

"Yes sir, you have and that's just the point. You've invested some six hundred days already, and with that kind of investment, you ought to be willing to add thirty days to ensure some kind of return. Any alternative would be sheer folly, and you folks don't look like no fools to me." This receives universal acclaim and the motion carries.

Next is a proposed ordinance allowing the hunting of all game, including people, in certain areas of the city to be announced daily in the newspaper. The author believes the ordinance would add a lot of excitement to city life while increasing commerce. This one is shelved while a committee looks into the economic potential.

There follows a series of ordinances in praise of this or that. Mrs. Gravatti then asks to be heard from the audience concerning the amount of praising present in the sessions.

Mrs. Gravatti is a retired sumo wrestler and comes to every council meeting to speak her mind. Many think the license to kill ordinance is designed with Mrs. Gravatti in mind.

"There's been too much praising," states Mrs. Gravatti. "The Lord cannot abide an excessive praiser and that's a fact. In Corinthians, it is said that the Lord loves a closet praiser, and does not put much stock in public praising. Every member of this council would praise the devil if he put more than a hundred dollars in their campaign fund." At this point there are a number of "amen sisters" from the audience. Mr. Lemme is writing something down, probably a reminder to put the devil on his campaign contribution list.

Mrs. Gravatti is getting a second wind. She puts on her Viking helmet, sings a little Wagner and gets ready to make the blood eagle. "I'm saying to hell with praise. This is a town that needs some vilifying. There's not a member of this council that couldn't use some good, clean, Christian vilification." Here she stops as the cries of "vilify them mothers" from the crowd have drowned her out.

Finally they get to our grant. I have spent forever developing my presentation and thinking of every argument and statistic needed to do battle. This whole thing is a damn honor.

"Is this thing about alkies?" asks Mr. Lemme. "Yes sir," I answer. Mr. Lemme ignores me and calls for a vote. It passes unanimously and Mrs. Gravatti has fallen asleep.

POPCORN TRANSMIGRATIONS

There is a fog outside my window and I can hear dragons in the distance. I can also hear Mr. Slids talking. "Do you think she is going to be alright? She is not really that messed up. I am really sorry about all this. I don't know what happened. I didn't mean to have an affair with her. My lord, she could be my daughter. Do you think I should see her?" No, I sure as hell do not. Mr. Slids is one of our most prominent county commissioners. In our neighborhood this means he can count past ten with only minor inconvenience.

His victim is eighteen years old and tried to commit suicide with an overdose of Valium. She met the commissioner when she was a high school intern for the commission. Mr. Slids explained he was not going to leave his wife and three children for the victim, and she responded with an overdose.

I also thank the victim will pull out of this with only minimal damage. The best treatment tool would be a wallet sized photo of Mr. Slids in the nude. Mr. Slids looks like a hairy turnip without the warmth and nutritional possibilities. If she looks at this from time to time, all the future will seem brighter.

Mr. Slids is a personal friend of Dr. Mondriatus and the victim came to us with no fanfare, *sub rosa*. She is being treated under another name and the press have so far not found her. I would like to help them out on this one, but the damage to the victim far outweighs the joy of watching Mr. Slids squirm.

On my desk there are two kernels of popcorn, one popped and one not. Every day I look at these miracles, and ponder the infinite magic that is all around me. How can the one come from the other? How are such things possible? We take this miracle of change for granted and yet there is no real explanation for this awesome transmigration. How is this huge, fluffy, white cloud held inside the armored kernel. I know, it involves the heat applied to the moisture in the kernel, but this in no way explains the miracle. How can you live in a world of such design and not see, even in this small kernel, that there is endless hope.

Because of Mr. Slid? How will he transmogrify? Into what will he change? If we put Mr. Slid in a large, covered skillet with enough oil . . .

THE WHITES OF THEIR EYES

"Do you know you can tell a great deal about people from the whites of their eyes ?" asks Mr. Milpody as he looks deeply into the whites of my eyes. Before I cannot respond, he goes on, "Healthy people, both spiritually and physically, have very clean whites." I concentrate on not pulling out my supply of Visine.

"The whites of my eyes are very clean because I have given up sin and red meat. It was really no problem. No problem at all. I am seeing more clearly since I gave these things up. Someone explained all this to me, but I cannot remember who it was or when. It wasn't very long ago, I think. I never saw God before I saw amphetamines. I have seen Him many times since then. He has a great sense of humor. Anybody who could make a duckbilled platypus and amphetamines has got to have a sense of humor. Do you believe in predestination? I believe in predestination because I was predestined to believe in it. I am unable not to believe in it, although I would like to not believe in it. What else could I be? I bet you have done a few drugs. That's what I bet and I'm a betting man." I quickly squeeze off a Valium and return to *Symbols in Transformation*.

"No one can act any other way than what they act. I have to do the things I do. I cannot not do them. Do you believe in random hits? Do you believe that some protons just move from point "A" to point "B" with no apparent cause? I think of killing people a lot. I dream of it. Is it not predestined that I kill someone? Maybe you." I gently finger the Colt Goldcup underneath my desk and think of the predetermination of the bullet to pass from point "A" to point "B" with only Mr. Milpody as a random possibility in its path. Do bullets dream?

Mr. Milpody fingers his prayer shawl and whittles away on the corner of my desk with a Swiss Army knife. He can not do otherwise. "Have you looked into God's eyes, doctor? I have looked into His eyes many times. His whites are growing ever more cloudy and He cannot do otherwise."

AND HE TOO SHALL ARISE

I have just finished staff development. Dr. Hilariat has presented a paper he found in the *Bronx Medical Journal*. It apparently has something to do with blood alcohol levels in intoxicated Eskimos, and the differences between their response times on a standardized test, and the response times of intoxicated subjects indigenous to the Bronx. I believe Dr. Hilariat was experiencing some blood alcohol levels himself when he found this puppy. He fell asleep during part of his presentation, but no one was left awake to tell him. Rumor has it that he once fell asleep while having sex with Nurse Akbar the Petulant, but this is also understandable.

While I eat my Payday candy bar, I look out the window which creates the aquarium for the patients roaming down below in our pastoral concrete meadow. One of them is urinating on a trash can. No one seems to notice. The two behavioral technicians are urinating on the other garbage can and cannot be bothered by this unauthorized patient urination. From time to time one of the grazing herd of patients is picked by a behavior tech to go to an assigned therapy session, like some beast of the field singled out for slaughter.

One has been singled out for me, Dr. Unnobody. He is part of our service to clinicians in the community. They seek salvation within their own profession, and are of course ostracized for their troubles. It is alright to have massive emotional problems, but it is not alright to admit it if you are one of us. Grown clinicians do not admit such frailties, they just self-medicate and pretend. This is perfectly acceptable. If, however, you are foolish enough to believe your own rhetoric about the whole thing just being another illness, like a viral infection, you are doomed. Everyone here knows it is a weakness of will. I love this place.

Dr. Unnobody graduated from Harvard and has been having a hard time since. His car looks just like him. It was the first car ever made and is kept in perfect running condition, but there are no frills attached. Jesus drove this baby when He lived in Nazareth. There is a writing pad and pencil attached to the dash. It has a schedule of the maintenance times for the vehicle and everything that has ever been done to it.

Dr. Unnobody enters the room. There is an umbilical cord attached to him that leads back to his car which is kept running at all times. The doctor was once kidnaped by aliens from space, but they returned him in fifteen minutes, and promptly went to the library where they destroyed all the copies of *War of the Worlds.*

"Your recreational services for patients leave a lot to be desired," states Dr. Unnobody and leans back in his chair while adjusting his umbilical cord. "If I was running this place, I could make a number of changes," states the good doctor. I think I liked him better when he originally came to our hallowed grounds. He had been on a ten day binge and whined and fawned a lot. I like that in a patient.

While driving his lovely car under the influence, he stopped at a local service station. After blowing the horn and cursing, he left the car to look for an attendant. A policeman in a nice blue uniform chose this time to come out of the restroom door. Dr. Unnobody promptly turned to him and stated, "Filler up, you stupid son-of-a-bitch," and the rest is history. This was his third DUI, and his lawyer knew it was time for him to become an impaired professional. Having this magical attribute is much like seeking sanctuary within the sacred clime of the church during the ages when people actually believed in the sacred clime of the church. Of course, I would have taken the same refuge, but it's so much fun to have the other guy fall in the shit. Dr. Unnobody is a difficult man to love. He is full of frailties, but none of them can be cuddled and petted. It's like dancing with a hippopotamus wearing a porcupine robe.

"Why is Dr. Mondriatus not seeing me personally," asks Dr. Unnobody. "I would think, under the circumstances, that I would be assigned to Dr. Mondriatus," he states and straightens his umbilical cord. "I'm afraid Dr. Moriatus died quite suddenly last Friday, but I'm relatively sure he would have preferred to see you given the two alternatives," I state while maintaining my most professional facade. "Should he come back to life, and his family does have a genetic history of rising from the dead, I shall notify him of your concern. And now, I'm afraid I'm late for my daily barium enema and must be on my way." I shall pay for this dearly, but I have placed a rainbow in my mind, and this is not to be discounted.

THE ZEN OF ZINFENDEL

"Have you never wondered why the Japanese have a wine named after a religion? Do you know the Yo-Yopanishads and the Zen of Then? Is the word Buddha just a corruption of the word Bubba and is this the front of back to the future again? There are diabolical games afoot and the doctor waits." No, Mr. Krillets, I have never pondered this one. I am into Manyana Zen and Tawdry Zen which opposes the yin of Fen Shui and makes the world a better place to live.

Mr. Krillets has lived in a lava lamp ever since the sixties. He and his lovely flower child wife have raised two children by accident. The children responded well to the call for love and doing their own thing. They are urban terrorists who are sucking the life blood from the Krillets. Mr. Krillet is now in the beginning of what is known as a psychotic break. Mr. Krillet has had enough.

Two days ago, Mr. Krillet found out that he had $8,220 in bills for online services. He also found out that it was his two lovely children, Whomp and Little Scout, who had run up the bills. He put on some Joan Baez, smoked some fine reefer, put all the children's toys in the garage and burned it to the ground. When the police and firemen arrived he was out front in some bell-bottoms screaming, "Burn, baby, burn." The police brought him to us because everyone who is caught wearing bell-bottoms in a public place ends up here.

A number of our clinicians have looked with envy upon Mr. Krillets' bell-bottoms and asked where they can get a new pair. Mr. Krillets has been unable to respond with any sensible directions, but these lads do not give up easily. Mr. Krillets will divulge his secret access code before he leaves this place. It never ceases to amaze. Half of our staff live in lava lamps, too, and have children much like Mr. Krillets. If only Mr. Krillets knew he was not alone.

We lied to Mr. Krillets when we told him that children would always go toward the light. For heaven's sake, Mr. Krillet, why do you think it takes eighteen years to raise the little twits? It takes a long time and a lot of discipline, consistency, and demands for excellence to make them vaguely human. What do you expect if you let them do whatever they want to do? They will be little animals with the empathetic understanding of a rock if you do not teach them what they should be. Whomp and Little Scout should just be recycled. They would make excellent lava lamps.

The children curse like drill instructors and have the manners of pigs. There is not enough reefer in the world to make life bearable with these toads. "The world needs love like it needs another comet to hit the Carribean. Screw the Zen in Zinfendel. Screw the Zen in xenophobia and screw the cap back on my mind and be damned, damned and thank you ma'am."

Mr. Krillets is taking a well deserved rest. Mrs. Krillets seems quite awed by the whole experience and keeps repeating, "It's the diet, he needs a strict organic diet." Luckily enough Mrs. Krillets has not shared one of our delicious hospital trays filled with food sent to us by the Albanian army. If Ms. Krillets finds out about Mr. Krillets' present diet she will divorce him because there are some past possibilities that cannot be overcome even with a strict organic diet. Wait, how strict is a strict organic diet and does this involve whips and chains? If so, possibly there is hope for Mr. Krillets if the whips and chains can be used on Whomp and Little Scout.

GOD'S CORNFLAKES

I always enjoy my sessions with Mr. Tenner. He is a twenty-three year old male Caucasian appearing his stated age. He has been appearing his stated age for many years. He is well dressed and well groomed and crazy as hell.

For five years Mr. Tenner did a gram of speed a day. Then one morning he woke up in bed with himself and was sobered by the experience. He has a cat named Albuquerque who was neither pleased not displeased by the event.

Mr. Tenner lives with his father and attends a local university. He is majoring in psychology and making straight "A's." I have been seeing Mr. Tenner for outpatient therapy for three months and he has been seeing me for the same period of time.

He is about six feet three inches tall with a soft voice that always sounds startled by itself. "I tried to talk with my father this morning," states Mr. Tenner to a corner of the room. Mr. Tenner's father has never said a kind word to him. For a long, long time, and even before, he has tried to please his father and to draw from him the attention he craves. He has tried being very good. He has tried being very bad in a clumsy kind of way. All have been dismal attention getters. "I think I've tried them all, Red Rider, if you get my drift," and Mr. Tenner spins both six-guns and drops them too cool back into their holsters.

If only Mr. Tenner could see what he is, and what potential exists. I can not seem to make the magic necessary to accomplish this feat. He is a lovely being, Mr. Tenner. Kind and gentle and intelligent and generous and humorous and without guile is Mr. Tenner, and he lives as a pimply, unimportant castaway from his father's thoughts. I love you, Mr. Tenner, and mean you well, but I cannot find the key to all these doors.

Mr. Tenner looks at his hand as if a scroll of words was unfolding upon it. "I asked my father if he believed in prayer while sitting at his

The Weeds of God

breakfast table. He was behind the newspaper hiding. He did not say anything for about half a day. Then he lowered the newspaper till just his eyes where alive in my distance. Everything grew very dark and someone was playing something by Bach. He said, "I believe in prayer so damn much that every damn day I pray that I can believe in God, you inadequate cornflake eating pansy." "But I wasn't eating the cornflakes anymore," says Mr. Tenner as he eats the rest of his cornflakes from the silver chalice upon the floor.

THE PRESENT PRESENT

The rain searches for passage through my window on the world. I ride with Rommel towards Tobruk with Bobbie's body next to mine and those window-shield wipers finding bits of old remembered time. It is distance. A great distance separates me and the present present of time. I would wander here yet a while, but the knock is upon the door.

Mr. Glidshall enters wearing a leather coat, goggles and a light coat of grease. He will not surrender to the Allies without a fight. I envy him his place in time.

"I am here and you may proceed," states Mr. Glidshall. "I have thought about what you said. I have thought and thought. Let us meander together through the maze of my problems. My voices are my saints. They are my direction posts. I can hear them more than I hear you. Time and time again they have saved me and you. They are most certain. Very certain. I could not find myself without them. They abound when they are needed. I know what I must do. They have told me to fall amongst you, all of you and your lies. The breakfast was cold again this morning." I could agree that I heard the same voices concerning the breakfast, but I remain the coy skeptic in a world of believers. Mr. Glidshall gets up and walks around his chair doing the famous Octawhapaho crane dance.

The hospital paging system states, "Code green, code green, code green." Mr. Glidshall looks slyly at me pondering the possibilities. Possibly an indication that a particular group of Mohammed's followers have attacked the hospital? A sect of rabid environmentalists have invaded the hospital atrium with signs reading, *Free the Bi-Polars*, believing them to be an endangered species of sexually confused bears?

"Ossian comes on waves of green his massive madness to redeem," states Mr. Glidshall as he dances around his chair. " They have spoken and their word is law. We all know them. Even the heathen knows them from his dreams and the voices that direct. We are the furrows

The Weeds of God

they plow with their wasted time. I am their's and my might is swift and to the point. Nothing comes, nothing goes, that is not in them and of them, and that's a damn fact Jack. There is blood in the tears they weep for us and sadness in the deeds that must be done and done again for we are the weeds of God. Everyone must pay the piper, but the piper has the most to pay." I think I am catching the drift of this one. We are discussing insurance companies and their hold upon the clinicians of the sacred grove.

"Shit," states Mr. Glidshall. Some truth has emerged. He stares out the window at Rommel's staff car parked at the curb. "You always kill the things you love. I have nothing to kill, not even most of all myself. What is this shit? What is this shit? What is this shit? Why is this shit?"

SMALL PEOPLE AND SMALL GUILTS

The day is long and frivolous. Days have passed since the hour hand changed its position. When they tell me I have two weeks to live, I will come here and spend a comfortable eternity. People in every hospice unit in the world should be heading here.

Somehow Friday is the longest day of the week. There is only one more patient to see, Mr. Guilford. He is extremely depressed. We know this because he told us. Usually we will not believe you, but we made an exception with Mr. Guilford because he donated one million dollars to the university and only asked for a plaque.

He has had no weight gains or losses, no sleep disturbance, no somatic symptoms, and no other secondary indications of depression. The psychometric evaluation indicates no depression. Our best diagnostic tool here is the local newspaper. It indicates Mr. Guilford is under investigation for fraudulent stock trading.

The six large market quotation machines sitting regally in the corner of my office suddenly come to life and Mr. Guilford enters. He is a large balding man with many things to say. "This is shit," says Mr. Guilford and sits in his large, custom made, leather chair. Something from Wagner is playing in the background and out my window you can see a vast industrial complex spewing massive and continuous layers of pollution into the atmosphere. Was Marx right? Was he a communist? Is he really buried in England? What does his psychometric evaluation indicate?

"I'm telling you, this is shit." I nod my agreement. For once I feel totally satisfied with our decision. "People who can't make shit are always afraid of people like me who can make millions from nothing. The little bastards are always nipping at my heels. They envy me and they are going to try to get me any way they can. Since they can't make shit, they don't want anyone else to either, the little shits. They are little people who sit around in little rooms in cheap suits trying every way they can to screw me because they are a bunch of impotent bastards."

Let us not clintonize the issue by making the truth tawdry, obfuscating it, and eviscerating its purveyors. There are a lot of references here, if I'm not mistaken, to fecal matter and impotence. I really need to take a break and peruse a little Freud and Jung. I also need to buy an expensive suit.

"Every trader cheats a little. There isn't a soul in the business who has not done it. That's a fact. Everyone knows it. What, you don't try to find out all the information you can and use the information to make money? Damn right you do. Every one trades information. How the hell could I make money? What, I've got some kind of genie in a bottle that tells me which stocks to buy and sell? Horseshit! I listen everywhere I can and I trade in information more than I trade in stocks. You can trust me. You give me information and I give you information. We both make money. Anyone in the business will tell you that Abe Guilford is a man of his word." I know Mr. Guilford. We all cheat a little and in doing so "the accepted" makes Swiss cheese of integrity. I am cheating Mr. Guilford. I know your mild depression is situational in nature and that you just want a place to hide. I know and I cheat too, but I tell myself, like you, that it is no big thing and hide from my own sight. I am afraid you may want me to testify that you are impaired, however, and there I will draw the line for I am a little shit too, but I will accept some good stock tips for my aging mother in Toledo. There is a smell of tawdry in the air and I must soon seek solace or perish.

DEMON RUM KICKS ASS

"I don't know why I can't stop. I know it all comes from the drinking. I drink to be exciting. It seems I say the funniest things when I've had a few. I've had some great times, but then it just has a mind of its own. It's a process that just keeps going, it becomes more than me. I know I can't control it. I even know I'm going to do it again. I know that much," states Mr. Millipod as he fingers his rosary beads made from deflated volleyballs.

Mr. Millipod becomes more than exciting when he is drunk. He also becomes violent and incoherent. Mr. Millipod is a thirty-two year old male Caucasian who appears younger than his stated age and is oriented to time, place, and person. His hospital number is DH4798653 and he has it tattooed on his right forearm. Mr. Millipod also played pro football for five years, and he is having problems forgetting the good times.

He frequents every sports bar in the city exploring his history of good times and having other people spend his money. Many are the great stories told about Mr. Millipod. He once urinated on a large screen TV image of Roger Staubach during a showing of the super bowl at his favorite sports bar. Mr. Millipod does not remember most of the funny things he does when he is drunk, but there is always someone around to tell him. They leave out all the sad parts, and make more of the small moments of joy than they will ever be. Mr. Millipod knows this, but he is willing to forget this tiny reality whenever he is given the chance.

"I know Katie is tired of all this. She's left me again, but I know she will be back. I miss my kid, he's everything. He's playing junior ball and he's going to be better than I was. He really knocks them on their ass. He put a kid out the other day for five minutes. She hasn't let him even call me. She'll be back. I know that. She just gets tired. She will not drink with me anymore. You know, we used to go out together and have the best times in the world. I mean, we had the best times in the world. Now she will not even touch a drop. She hasn't called yet, but I know she'll come around. I wrote her like you suggested, but I know she'll come around. We've been through this a hundred times or more, and she always comes around. I mean, there is no one else or anything, she's just mad at me." Mr. Millipod fingers his probowl ring. He turns it around and around. The stadium crowd is his. They know she will come back. She is just mad. Women are like that sometimes. They do not understand what this is all about.

"I've got to talk with Butch. I've got to let him know his father loves him and will be home soon. I know he would have called if she let him. No father and son are closer than we are to each other. I've been teaching him how to play ball since he could walk. He's really going to be great. We watch all my old games together. He loves it. He loves his old man. I know he's proud of me. I've heard him telling the other kids what a great player I was. You know how good that makes me feel? It makes me feel great. I know he would have called if she would have let him." Mr. Millipod pulls off his helmet. Dirt and blood have streaked his face. His eyes stare into the distance of the next play and all he will have to give to be his best. The game, alas, has changed. Size and speed mean little. DEMON RUM KICKS ASS.

"She says he was frightened. I don't remember, but it can't be that bad. She says I was covered with vomit and I pissed on the carpet in the living room. She says I cursed her and Butch. She says I picked Butch up and shook him. I know I wouldn't hurt my kid. I know I would never do anything like that. She says I fell over the coffee table and couldn't get up. It couldn't have been that bad. I don't remember, but I think she's just trying to scare me. I don't think it was that bad. I mean, it wasn't good, but I don't think it was that bad. Everybody gets drunk some times. I don't think it was that bad." DEMON RUM KICKS ASS.

"Did you know that five slave states fought on the side of the North? Missouri, Maryland, Kentucky, Delaware and West Virginia fought for the North. Did you know that Lincoln stated on numerous occasions that he would never fight a war over slavery and that the only reason to go to war was to preserve the union? Did you know that the Emancipation Proclamation only freed slaves in states that refused to rejoin the Union? Did you know Lincoln stated that the Emancipation Proclamation was his most difficult decision? He did it because the North was losing the war and he thought it would cause a slave revolt in the South. Did you know that the vast majority of those who fought for the South owned not one slave. Did you know that Garibaldi was offered the command of Union troops, but refused because Lincoln categorically refused to state that the war was over slavery. Did you know that the majority of Southern troops fought only because they saw their country being invaded? Did you know that the South was looted, pillaged and humiliated by the North during Reconstruction? Did you know that 30,000 Tennesseans fought for the North during the war? My great-great-grandfather was one of those 30,000." Yes, I know. I know, Mr. Facade, but it was long ago, and not the important point in the present circumstances. General Lee feeds Traveler a carrot. General Lee has refused to accept Mr. Facade's sword.

"My daughter is not responsible for her actions. I still don't believe she did it. She must have been on drugs or something. It's just not possible. It's not possible. A bad dream." Mr. Facade begins to cry. General Lee puts his hand on Mr. Facade's shoulder and feeds him a carrot.

Mr. Facade's daughter killed her child. She gave her daughter an eternal sleep of Percodan. Mr. Facade's daughter has not moved or spoken since the death of the child. She is catatonic. She has left her building and no longer wishes to return. She is with us to be evaluated to stand trial. If she is sane, the state can find her guilty, and provide a lethal injection because we hate sanity in this state.

Mr. Facade's daughter had a child by a black man, and she had never even read the Emancipation Proclamation. I have seen the child only in death, but she was quite lovely. Somehow the best of both races seems to be held here in this small broken life. What would she have been and what feats accomplished?

"You know she was crazy at the time. She wouldn't harm anyone. She was so gentle. You have got to know this for God's sake. You must know. This is all crazy." Yes, Mr. Facade, it is all crazy. It is all crazy.

She did not know what to do. The man who gave her the child could not love her or care for her, and she was hopeless, so hopeless. You stood up for her having the child. You were at her side when her lover was gone. You always believed and fought for equality between races and religions and ethnic groups. You were outspoken in your beliefs and you backed them up.

But, there was something in your eyes, as even now, that betrayed your words. Was it the immediacy of the genetic pool?

She needed you so and you blinked. It was not that you rejected her or the child, it was her realization that it was an intellectual position you would have taken in a debate. This, however, was not a debate and she needed you, not the integrity of your ethical stance. She needed to see in your eyes that she, and her child, were one with you, not one with your conception of good taste. General Lee prepares to send the Texas Brigade up another hill, knowing the finality of the act and being totally committed to it.

The bits and pieces of your daughter are scattered as shattered glass. I do not know if anyone can put them back together. The drugs only help by stopping all meaning, all meaning. This is what she seeks, the cessation of all meaning for all meaning leads to one small child in death.

General Lee talks with Jackson. Jackson goes to stand by her and his eyes are clear and dedicated to his task. He stands like a stonewall because sometimes only a stonewall will suffice.

DR. PHUSTUS AND ROGET

We, the masters of psychic vivasection, set regaling ourselves in the hidden parts of our favorite bar. Everyone knows that we are harmless, and ignore our momentary lapses of courtesy and good manners. And we are great tippers, all but Dr. Phustus. Dr. Phustus has never paid a bar bill in his life, preferring to believe that his company is pay enough and he is frequently right. Dr. Phustus is a tall, dysplastic man with a glass eye and always carries a copy of *Roget's Thesaurus* which he uses for toilet paper. "Let me tell all of you something," states Dr. Phustus as he stabs the air with the three middle fingers of his right hand as if he were a magician about to turn all of us into princes, "I do that for a reason. When I was a child we were dirt poor, I mean dirt poor. You never understand, because you don't know shit about dirt poor, but we were dirt poor." At this time a large neon sign over the table begins to flash *He was dirt poor, He was dirt poor*, and a haunting gypsy melody is played by a small child with an ocarina. Dr. Phustus backhands the small gypsy child, and states, "I mean it when I say dirt poor. I used newspaper to wipe my ass until I was sixteen years old. Now I wipe may ass with some damn class. You see what I'm saying. Can any of you assholes catch this stuff? Do you see the Hegalian logic of the thing? And I am not an anal retentive and I'm ashamed of one of you for saying it too." I fondle my copy of *Symbols in Transformation* and head for the bathroom.

Dr. Commradius looks sideways from beneath his crumpled hunting hat at Dr. Phustus and states, " Now brother, you know we all love you and it's just his way of making fun." Dr. Commradius is a large man in every way there is to be a large man. Whenever he enters a room, he brightens even the darkest corners. He always seems to see some good in all the bad that he sees, but he can not see the immense joy he gives the world in which he lives. "That's it, that's exactly what I'm talking about," states Dr. Phustus and stabs the air again vainly attempting to turn us into princes. "Ye who have eyes but will not see are cursed to fill the night with darkness. You refuse to see what is right in front of your eyes. I have risen above ego, I have metamorphasized into something that you do not comprehend. I can see that I am the most intelligent person I have ever known. I can see this with humility. Some of you are almost as intelligent as I am and I can see that, for it was given to me to see such things, but I do not suffer fools easily. And that's a fact."

"Excuse me, but the adumbrations of godliness, was that before you fell and hit your head, or do you believe it added fifty IQ points to your possibility," I state while encouraging the gypsy child to play "Lilli Marlene." I love that damned song. "You see, that's what I'm saying," states Dr. Phustus. I interrupt to say," You are saying you gained fifty IQ points after the fall?" "No, you ass, I am telling you that you are not attending to the magnitude of what is presented to all of us. You have missed the point and seem unable to return though I show unto you the way, you rapscallion." A neon sign over the table lights up, *Dr. Phustus Died For Your Sins.* "Turn that shit off or I will crucify you, you spawn of a minor equation, you wart on God's ass," states Dr. Phustus. The sign goes off. "I interrupted myself and this should be the only possibility. I am God's own diagnostician. I see behind the veil. I have been to Plato's cave and left the wiser unlike lesser men and I know the truth behind the rose." At this point Dr. Pharnakar, who has been silently contemplating his navel and hoping for a point in the conversation, falls head first on the table. Dr. Phustus makes a sweeping gesture over Dr. Pharnakar's head with his right hand. "Have I not said unto you that God would send us a sign? This, my beloved, is written. This is God's way of showing us the direction we must follow." "You mean God wants us to pass out?" I state, while replacing Dr. Phustus copy of *Roget's Thesaurus* with my copy of *Symbols in Transformation.*

SHADOWS

My office is full of shadows. I can see the mountains of the moon in the distance, and hear a waterfall hidden behind the door to the chart room. I hope the drain is working.

If we evolved from the ocean, why can't I breath underwater? Wait. I have never tried to breath underwater. Maybe I should let Mr. Ellis-From try it first. I do not wish to hoard this discovery. I should share it with Mr. Ellis-From. We were ocean apes chased out by larger carnivores into the light of this blue air world. Some of us must have made it, and immediately started to copulate. The same old story.

Mr. Ellis-From knocks on my door. "Good morning, fellow ocean ape," says Mr. Ellis-From and winks at me with his one good eye. "It is nice to have someone other than your family wake you up at all hours of the morning. It is nice to know that strangers can be as inconsiderate as family. I think this is a nice thing to know," states Mr. Ellis-From. "Do you do this to put us under tension, so we will reveal more in these incredibly exciting sessions? Do you know you don't talk much? I know, I am supposed to talk and you are supposed to listen. Maybe there is not any reason why I do the things I do. Maybe I like heroin because it makes me feel very good. In fact, it makes me feel damn wonderful. I cannot think of anything bad when I am full of the lovely white lady of dreams. I bet you have tried some too. You just can't tell me about it because it would put a hole in our already shaky relationship. Right?"

Yes, you are right Mr. Ellis-From, but I do not think I will tell you anyway for there is so little to say about the stuff of dreams. "I no longer find my wife sexually attractive," states Mr. Ellis-From. "She is beautiful, but my dreams are even more beautiful. Nothing is as beautiful as my dreams, but I cannot remember them. I just remember their beauty. I do not remember anything sad, except when the white lady has drifted away. Sadness falls all around when she has gone. I have heard that people physically ache for those they love, but I never knew this reality until I found the lady. I must devote all my time to her." Mr. Ellis-From looks at me and through me to his memories setting like filing cabinets of time. "There is such a passion to this beast that is always consuming its own beauty. It dissolves into itself and returns. I must always chase it and that makes it even more valuable."

TEN KLICKS OUT

Mr. Hamsung walks carefully on the paddy dike looking for any anomalies on the ground. There is a smell of dung and a slight breeze from the sea. There is a village in the distance with bunkers and all manner of interesting possibilities. He steps off the paddy dike and sits in his chair. He places his 782 gear around him waiting for moments to come.

"So what's up, doc?" asks Mr. Hamsung. I fire a burst into the tree line - recon by fire. "I should have stayed in the Corps. Civilian life is shit. I can't remember why I got out. No, I remember. Betty wanted to stay in one place. Well, we are sure as hell staying in one place. I can't hold a job for more than a month. We must have lived in six shitty places in the past five months. I can't take the crap they give you. Funny, I used to say "sir" to all manner of assholes, but it wasn't the same somehow. I don't know. I know both of you think I'm not trying, but I am. I am trying. I'm tired of hearing what morons who were not there think about the war. Sometimes I feel tired all the time, like I had run some kind of race and lost." Mr. Hamsung is cleaning his M-16.

It's ten klicks out
And ten klicks back
With an M-16
And a marching pack

With a combat load
And a little C-4
We come calling
At Charley's door

"I don't know how to act anymore, and my skills seem a might wasted. Everybody knows how to act, but me. That dispatcher job; I kept hearing things on the radio that were not there. I knew not to give call signs and such, but I thought I heard them calling. Maybe they were calling. I did two tours, but I should have stayed. I left a lot of people in that place."

Morning Mr. Charley
How you been
The 3rd Marines
Have just dropped in

Don't trouble yourself
Just the usual fare
Some 155's
And on call air

"I keep reading how we lost the war. What war did we lose? We kicked their ass. They never won even one damn battle. Well, they did get the hearts and minds of the American people, right. I hate the damn press. I don't know anybody over there who didn't hate most of them. The '68 Tet offensive was a disaster for them, but the press acted as if they had won. Must have been a hell of a surprise for the slopes."

Morning Mr. Charley
Here's some WP
To crank your handle
And set you free

If I die
In a combat zone
Bag me up
And ship me home

Take my Zippo
And my four canteens
My old steel pot
And my cammo greens

Hand them down
To an FNG
When he cranks one off
Remember me

"Why does everyone hate us so much? I didn't kill any babies. Most of the time I can't even figure out what the hell they are mad at us about. I wish I had never left the damn place. Nothing here seems to make any sense. Sometimes I think it was safer over there than it is over here. I had friends over there. I don't even know who my friends are over here. It's just no good. I can't figure out what to do to make the damn thing work." A large mushroom of napalm rises from the bunker complex. Looks like crispy critters for breakfast, Gunny.

SATURDAYS GONE

"I think this thing is being blown out of all proportion. Everybody has a drink once in a while for God's sake. I'm the bread-winner in my home. My wife doesn't have to hit a lick. I mean she's back teaching school now, but that's because she wants to do it. I don't want her to, but it seems my fall from grace has left her in charge. It's not like the old days when everyone was my big buddy. Everyone wanted tickets to the game. I used to get her mother twenty tickets to every game, every game. Now that woman won't even talk to me. I still haven't talked to my son. I know he's hurt and I know he wants to call me. He needs his old man." Mr. Millipod looks at the empty playing field. Where are all the cheering ghosts of Saturdays gone. "Do you believe what you said, Mr. Millipod?" I ask and pass off the ball to the fullback. "What do you mean?" "Do you believe your son needs you?" That is what I mean Mr. Millipod.

"Of course he needs me. We are buddies. I'm always there for him. I mean, sometimes I make a mess of it, but not often. I still sell more bonds than almost anyone in this berg. I buy him anything he wants. I go to every little league game. His coach doesn't know garbage. I mean, he played at UT for heaven's sake. He never played pro ball for even a day. He can't cut it. They need to get people that know what they are doing. I could do it, but they are jealous of me." "How much time do you spend with your son in the average week, Mr. Millipod?"

"Have you heard of quality time? That's what everybody tells me, quality time. That's what I spend with my son."

"Is quality time spent in vomiting in your living room, cursing and threatening your wife and shaking your child so hard you cracked one of his ribs?" I ask in my most neutral of tones. Mr. Millipod is quiet. The coach has grabbed his face mask. This game will last until his last breath. The important thing is the next play, that is the important thing. The responsibilities are different and nobody claps for you when you have made a great play except you. Mr. Millipod is thinking how much he would like a drink. I am thinking how much I would like a drink. I am thinking I have played this game before, and I am a sanctimonious bore. He needs some sanctimony, does Mr. Millipod and a hand upon his face mask with some darkening words within his ears that will not hear.

"That's one damn time. That's one stinking damn time, not every damn day. Maybe there were a few other times, but mostly it's good times. Why can't I celebrate when I've made a killing in the market? Everybody seems to line up for the money. Why can't I have a good time too? Most of the time I handle alcohol just fine. Maybe I should just drink beer. If I just drink beer, I wouldn't have any problems, but the stuff tastes like crap. Maybe that's what I'll do. I'll just drink beer and all this will be ended." Katie and little Butch are shaking their heads in the stands. Another bad play will not help. A small hand holds Mr. Millipod's face mask, "I need you daddy, I need you." Mr. Millipod hears and cries for what is lost, but he still looks to the stands and believes the next play will bring back the ghosts of Saturdays gone.

FORNICATORS ON FIVE

I have been summoned by the great one, He-Who-Must-Be-Obeyed. Seven secretaries guard the seven doors to his hallowed abode. At each portal those seeking audience must place their hand on the DSM and swear undying allegiance to the Grand Master of Psychic Vivisection. There is a large python who appears to be either asleep or dead stretched across the final portal. Here also is Ms. Gorgon with robes of black and great cat eyes. "Enter and find the wisdom you seek," states Ms. Gorgon and gives the python a playful kick with her jungle boots. I love this place.

I see Dr. Frustus in a distance through a shimmering mist. "I have need of you, young doctor. Do you know Dr. Usbacc? Of course you do. I need you to help him in his appointed rounds for a time. As you may or may not have heard he has been experiencing some slight difficulties. Have I made myself perfectly clear?" asks Dr. Frustus as a large raven lands on my shoulder. He-Who-Must-Be-Obeyed has made himself perfectly clear, and I acknowledge his clarity and wisdom while bowing myself out of his presence. The raven states, "There's more, there's more" and flies back into the mist. I shall miss that bird.

Yes, I know of Dr. Usbacc's slight difficulties. He has not drawn a sober breath since Jesus was a carpenter. He is also one of the most charming and gentle of beings. His only bout of aggression was the day on which he attempted to kill his father for having beaten the hell out of his mother a few hundred times. All six shots missed as Dr. Usbacc had imbibed two fifths of bourbon to steady his shooting hand. His father died of cancer before Dr. Usbacc had a chance to reload, and he has been the sadder for it low these many years.

I take the magical elevator to the fifth floor where Dr. Usbacc runs a unit for patients with all manner of entertaining psychoses. We have paranoid schizophrenics, chronic undifferentiated schizophrenics, borderlines, and an assortment of those who have crossed borders that most of us will only dream about. I make my way through the ever present darkening fog and open the portals with my sacred key. There is trouble in the place with a capital "T".

Dr. Usbacc's voice can be heard throughout the unit, " I am sick and tired of this shit. You people have got to stop fornicating on this damn unit. I will not abide any more continued fornicating on my unit, you fornicating bastards." Dr. Usbacc is addressing an assembled meeting of all the staff and patients. "Get this through your heads, no fornicating on my unit." "Dr. Usbacc, I wonder if I might see you for just a moment," I inquire in what I believe to be my most respectful voice. "Of course you can see me. Are you a damned blind person? No, you're some kind of psychologist. If you can't see me, you are sick and probably a fornicator too. Have you been drinking? That's ok, just sit back and listen to this and learn something about the business. Now, where was I before this blind bastard interrupted me? Right. Liz here is pregnant as hell and can't tell me who the father is because she has the syllogistic reasoning of a dead pigeon. Now, I'm just going to ask this once and I had better get some straight damn answers or there will be the devil to pay. Who on this damn unit has fornicated with Liz? I want you to raise your hands and I mean now. Raise your damn hands if you have fornicated with Liz. Nurse Edwards, take down their names." There is a slight pause and then every male patient and two of the female patients raise their hands for a total of twenty-seven people. There is a pounding on the seclusion room door. Mr. Clites, a seventy-five year old with Huntington's chorea and paranoid schizophrenia, can be seen raising his hand through the glass observation window. That just about covers it for me.

THE WHITE COAT BLUES

"All my octaves died. Dead every one and how many times must a white dove fly before she sleeps in the sand. I need some blow for this wind. Lord, lord, I need some blow for where I've been and that's the blues, brother." Mr. Vinigal is at his best today. I am at my worst. The medical school residents have descended for their weekly introduction to the mysteries of our world. Thank God, none of them have any interest in becoming psychiatrists. There are five of them and you could not find a good canasta player among them. They have very large eyes, very large white coats and are ready to believe, if only someone will show them. I hate this damn stuff. I feel like I am showing off my trained seal. I always pick ones that really want to give the residents a treat, but it still seems tawdry and I have almost run out of sequins for my gown. Then again, Mr. Vinigal always volunteers for duty and seems to get more out of it than the residents.

"Around and around the around-and-around we go. Where we stop only the big toad knows." The residents are making notes. What the hell are they noting? No, I do not want to know. I have the feeling they want to shake Mr. Vinigal to see what new colors he can turn.

"Do you know who Jellyroll Morton is and why no flies come his way?" asks Mr. Vinigal of one of the residents. The resident looks to me. Play some Thelonius Monk and forget it. Mr. Vinigal is humming what he probably presumes is "Mack the Knife," but he seems to have it confused with "Claire de Lune."

Mr. Vinigal was brought in about an hour ago. He has enough heroin in his system to kill the average bear. Mr. Vinigal has played sax in some well known jazz bands, but the white lady has taken a bit of his wind and given him nothing but half-remembered dreams. The police know Mr. Vinigal very well and he is liked by one and all. When he looks like he is going to have a few problems, they just bring him home to us. We have worked with him for two years and never managed to keep him off the drugs for any longer than we hold him in our sacred grove. In other words, we have done about as much for him as the white lady. We get his jones down a little and straighten out some problems with his plumbing system. Yes, the white lady will constipate you just for the fun of it. All that and constipation too. It is Christmas every day in this place.

The residents have been told they can ask questions of Mr. Vinigal and interact in the supportive fashion they have been taught. "I play some jazz piano," states one of the residents. I bring the .45 out of my shoulder holster and put it to my head, but Mr. Vinigal has heard this one before. "No shit, Sherlock, you have made my day. White clad assholes of jazz piano fame come to give me shame. See you here, see you now, see you coming any how. More of the blues, man; I am giving more of the blues. Jesus, what an intellectual feast for you shits. Where the hell am I?" More notes are taken. Could it be Mr. Vinigal is not oriented to place? Is there not a certain *belle indeferance* present in our midst?

Mr. Crowley keeps his head down. He looks at the shabby parts of the past. He is a kind and gentle man to whom fate has been unkind. There is so much of him. He stands six feet ten inches tall and none of his parts seem to make a whole when he moves. The other children are still making fun of his inability to put all of himself into any concerted motion. He hears their laughter every day of his life.

Mr. Crowley does not go to bars and cause trouble. He does not betray anyone except the person he would be. Each night he sits at home and drinks until he passes out and the laughter dies. His employer, Mr. Gotman, loves him deeply. Each time he fails to come to work, Mr. Gotman goes and finds him at his home. He brings him to us that we may fix the broken parts of Mr. Crowley.

Mr. Crowley has no friends. His sister died six years ago. She too was large and gentle and rejected by the midgets who surrounded her. They were happy, the two of them, and played in the moon light where no one else could see. They talked of small things and laughed. They were the same size, you see, and never spoke of the deformities of others whom they knew. They were not alone then. But the wind from the ocean took this large Annabel Lee and all Mr. Crowley loved from the earth. The moonlight was empty of laughter, and he could write no poems to empty some small part of his grief and fears.

"He works hard. He's the best worker I ever had. It seems like you ought to be able to do something. This happens about every three months. I mean, he comes in with a hangover some other times, but he still works better than anybody I ever had in the place. You see, there ought to be some way to help him. I mean, I've tried, but it don't seem to do no good. I mean, I'll keep him forever, but I think maybe there's something wrong with him, you see," states Mr. Gotman.

Yes, Mr. Gotman, there is something wrong with him, you see. "Hey, ape boy, come over here and get some bananas." "It's the son of Frankenstein." Do not go out to play for the halflings have conquered the earth. They infest every corner of it.

He does not seem to know what a joy it would be to crush one of the little shits. I love you Mr. Crowley. I love you and I am useless to you. I can give you some rearranging of thoughts, but I cannot bring your sister back. You will still be all alone in a world of petulant, deformed midgets, you see.

FORMALLY OWNED BY A CULSWAMP

Mr. Culswamp enters in one of his red robes with a white drawstring accompanied by his introductory text to abnormal psychology. I have him on this one, because the text is an old one and I cannot even remember some of the stupidities it contains. "What would you like my soliloquy to be on today, young doctor? Shall I tell you why I never wanted to kill my father and have sex with my mother, or would you find some of my masturbation techniques and fantasies more rewarding?" I think seriously of calling a code black for three South and having Dr. Kervorkian appear to instruct Mr. Culswamp in suicide techniques. "What do you want to talk about, Mr. Culswamp?" I ask in the hopes he will request Dr. Kervorkian for his therapist.

"Shit. I do sometimes enjoy talking with you. I don't know why. At least you don't tell me your damn problems. Everyone has problems. I know. I drink to forget mine. Right? Maybe I do and maybe I don't. Everything does not have to have a reason why. I feel good when I drink. That is the reason I drink. Things do not look half so bad when I drink. I know, what are my problems? I think it is Memphis Malaise. I think I was happy in New York. You have no idea what a berg this is because you have never lived in New York. It's like steak. If the only thing you have ever eaten is beans and franks, you have no idea what you are missing. The problem is I have had the steak and now I have Memphis." Thousands of people appear at the door with airline tickets to New York for Mr. Culswamp. As I look out the window more than half of the city is down below waving airline tickets for Mr. Culswamp. I pull mine from the drawer and add it to the pile. There is a call from the Mayor of New York indicating that a lawsuit will be filed if Mr. Culswamp reappears, and offering to pay a thousand dollars a day if he remains in Memphis.

"Nothing seems to matter. I make money and I'm not happy. I have a nice house, a dog, a wife and a child in the best school in the city. Not that it compares with any really good school in New York, but it's the best here. I've got it made and so what. Nothing is really very interesting and nothing seems to make me happy. Nichavo." I write a note for Mr. Culswamp to be delivered to the slums of Buenos Aires for a three-month stay. A little beans and franks may direct his attention to the more important aspects of human existence. A call comes in from the mayor of Buenos Aires indicating they will up New York's offer by two thousand a day.

"My father knew all the best things. He ate in the best restaurants and he had all the things you would ever want. He had a Mattise in his living room, a damn good Mattise too." A call comes in from representatives of the Mattise estate offering to buy the painting for an astronomical sum with the understanding that Mr. Culswamp will never again state that his father owned it. Apparently dealers are now demanding that all such paintings have a stamp on them reading *Formally Owned by a Culswamp*. "It's the kiss of death, I can tell you," states the dealer.

THE GI BILL

The rain falls heavy upon the bunker. We are cleaning our weapons and thinking warm, fuzzy thoughts. "I'm going to stop drinking," states Mr. Hamsung and water drips, drips, drips down his poncho. "I mean it this time. I meant it every time. I don't want to hurt her anymore. Maybe I should just take my ass away. I love her and I trust her. She is the only friend I have." Mortar rounds explode in the distance muffled by the rain.

"What do you think I can do? She says I can do anything, but I just mess it up. I've got the GI Bill and I could continue in school, but there is not a damn thing I want to take. I looked at the curriculum, but I can't find anything I want to start. I can't even find anything I want to finish except maybe me. I think about killing myself a lot. I think of it almost every day, but I know what it would do to my parents and to her. It seems like the best thing sometimes. I don't feel like losing anymore. I just want everything to be right and I screw everything up. I'm nervous all the time except when I drink. I'm nervous because I know I will screw it up. When I drink, I think great thoughts and the future is going to be great. The next day I feel like killing myself all over again. I know it can't keep going this way. I know that." The NVA moves into place around Khe Sahn and the rain does not care.

"Do you ever think about all the mistakes you have made? I do. I do that a lot. I should have stayed in the Corps. I knew how to do that. Nothing seems worth trying now. I know, I know I've got to try at least for her. I know that. I'm going to try hard. Sometimes I try to make sense of all of the things I've seen and it just seems to make it worse. I can't think it through. There is always an empty spot. It's like a road with a big empty in the middle of it that you can't get across." Two NVA sappers, Mo and Curley, plant a mine in the road and tap it down. There is a small explosion in the distance. I shall miss them for I think they had begun to make sense of it all.

MR. JAMES' STAIRS

Mr. James arrives in a flourish of trumpets heard from a great distance. He wears the crown of grass for he has saved his army this day. One of his shoes is larger than the other. Is this an affectation? "Greetings and may a big dog shit on your lawn. You like the sex, don't you. You want to know what it was like to be inside my sister. I have seen your eyes open at the dream of her, you old rowdy you. You must have had your sister too. I would like a poke at her myself. I'm an old cowpoke and I don't mind admitting it to a fellow traveler. My sister is nowhere to be found though, but she will return, just you wait and see somewhere over the rainbow." Mr. James removes some grass from his crown and smokes it in his pipe.

"I love every kind of drug God made. Why do you think they won't let us do drugs? They hate happiness, the puritanical bastards. They want everyone to be as dull and unhappy as they are. If it makes you happy, it must be the devil's work. That's what they believe. Look at the God they make up. He's mean as hell and everyone is scared of him. Their churches are quiet as if He would get mad if they had a good time. Black people have a kinder God. I have been in their churches and they are having a damn good time with Him. White people are just scared of Him. Why didn't we have any dessert for lunch today? Because it's too good for people. It makes you feel too good. I eat dessert when ever I want. My sister is dessert. She is my dessert. She is mine saith the Lord and He meant it too. He beat us all the time, but He gave us each other and that's a fact. Why must He take her away now?" Mr. James arranges the fold in his toga and looks at his red shoes. His hands are clasped reverently in front of him and he preys to some unknown deity in the distance.

Mr. James' father beat him and his sister when they were children. He beat them often, and they knew he would beat them always. He locked them in a closet for punishment. Sometimes they were in the closet for days. They sat in the darkness of their own excrement. They imagined themselves far away in a land where they held great power. In this land they could not be harmed and they could right the wrongs that had been done to them. They walked in valleys full of fallen rainbows and streams of clear, cool water. They dreamed within a single dream that reached as far as their desperation. They held each other dear, for nothing else could be held without fear. Then one day their father died. He fell down the stairs in the huge home full of closets in which they lived. He fell and fell down the stairs, and they knew what they had done.

DEAR JOHN

The sun hangs heavy on us from a clear sky. A Skyraider circles in the distance like a great hawk searching for prey. Mr. Hamsung has received no letters from his wife and his phone calls have gone unanswered. Have the Hated-Cong taken the position in this long night?

"She's really mad this time. I feel like some small child being punished. She's right. I know she's right. It all just starts with one. I never mean to drink more than one or two. That's the truth. The jukeboxes are deadly. I play a few tunes from the old times and I'm there again. I hear Petula Clark's "Downtown" and I'm in Nam again. I don't know why I miss it so. People got killed. I can remember them as if it happened yesterday. It's like a loose tooth when you were a child. I worry it back and forth, back and forth inside my mind. Maybe it's because I was so important. Maybe it's because it was so intense and you can remember every minute. Maybe it's because I'm nothing now and there is nothing for me here." Mr. Hamsung cleans his M-16 and smokes a Camel. We are between times of battles and the sun hangs heavy on us from a clear sky.

"Am I going to get out of this? I wonder. I really miss her. I mean to do well. I will do well. This can be overcome just like everything else. Ain't no big thing. Sometimes I feel so sad and I don't know why. Sometimes nothing seems right. Just a few words said by some asshole can send me off. I feel like killing them. I mean, I really would like to kill them and later I don't feel anything at all. The truth is I don't care what they think about the war. They are pogues and I really couldn't care less. Sometimes it's not about the war, I don't even know what it's about. I feel very angry. I feel like everyone has taken something from me." We are between times of battle and the sun hangs heavy on us from a clear sky.

Mrs. Hamsung has decided to get a divorce. I talked to her yesterday and my words fell empty at her feet. " I've got my own life to lead. My parents are afraid he will really hurt me. You hear all sorts of things about what they do. He never really talks about it, but I have heard all sorts of things on TV. One of them killed someone in Kentucky." They are not "thems" Mrs. Hamsung, they are your husband. Besides, there are plenty of people in Kentucky who need a little killing. Maybe it was justifiable homicide. Please, please try one more time and one more time again. He is far away now, but we can bring him home if you will help. If he finds your Dear John, I fear that he will never come home, for you are the only one left in the platoon. We are between times of battle and the sun hangs heavy on us from a clear sky.

DR. BABIKAL'S DIAGNOSIS

Lethargy drapes herself around my neck and gives me a large kiss. We are all in the penthouse listening to our weekly continuing education program. Dr. Babikal drones on across the continent of Africa. "Rommel Continues Drive to Egypt." Two physicians have died in the back from lack of water and constipated thought processes. They shall not be missed. We need all the water that is left for ourselves. Dr. Babikal drones on. We move as a group across the desert. I can see only sand as far as the eye can see. Can we really take Akaba?

"This is the very essence of retroactive inhibition," states Dr. Babikal as he points to a slide containing directions to the tomb of Tutankhamen. Everyone believes Dr. Babikal is the best diagnostician in the world. Dr. Babikal believes he is the best diagnostician in the world. Everyone prefers to see his written reports rather than listening to the nasal twang of eternity cast before you down all time. If anyone asks a question, I will kill them.

Dr. Tlaloc, the grand exalted assistant superintendent, sits in the front row staring raptly at the slide to which Dr. Babikal is pointing. Dr. Tlaloc graduated from Yale and he includes this in every paragraph he produces. Dr. Babikal also graduated from Yale. The similarities are obvious. Ten minutes with either one of them would convince you that there is no God. Any divinity that would produce such beings would be ridiculous. Two grand viziers of pomposity sitting in the same room. The cleaning crew must work for days to scour the pomposity off the walls and the floor after these lads have finished.

Wait a minute, I may have hit on something here. If the universe is fourteen billion years old, it may explain the whole dilemma. Surely even God would hit senility around ten billion years. I am in the midst of creation with a God Who has Alzheimer's. It continues to be interesting to Him because He cannot remember what the hell it was all about in the first place. Then why the hell hasn't Dr. Babikal found this out? Maybe Dr. Babikal is God.

The Weeds of God

Dr. Pokomiac the Blatantly Wise rises in his chair and states, "It is at this point that I must respectfully disagree, Dr. Babikal." Four of us rush forward, cover Dr. Pokomiac with a rug and throw him to the floor. Soon a herd of our small, strong ponies ridden by hard men from the steppes will ride over his body for he is a son of the Khan and we must not watch him bleed.

THE FALLS OF TIME

I am watching death and death is watching me. Dr. Contritus, one of my few great friends, is dying. His kidneys have decided to go on strike.

Dr. Contritus can make your day. He is someone you truly look forward to seeing. I would take him on a hill when there was no ammo left, only epithets for comfort, and a battalion of well armed necrophiliacs on the doorsteps. He would stay and be counted and there is nothing else. Nothing else.

Is it not amazing how few people you look forward to seeing, really look forward to seeing, like Christmas day when you were a small, innocent of life's demands, child. So few, and he is one of these and dying.

His disease is a fast-forward to death. What age would have wrought over forty years the disease spins out in forty days. Each day I see him, a year has passed and each day another. He sinks in upon himself. Soon he will consume the space between life and death and begin again. My loss will be unfathomable. I will miss him so.

Nothing will be quite as bright again. Within every future explosion of joy there will be the taste of his loss, every new sadness will be deepened, and the shadow of his absence will fall on all the infinite in-betweens.

Dr. Contritus is thirty-five years old and dying. The world is full of shits and God has picked Dr. Contritus. God is very busy. Surely this is obvious, but possibly I can help. Each night in my prayers I send unto God a listing of the shits I suggest should be harvested in the very near future. God needs this kind of help. I am one of God's clerks. Possibly God can substitute twenty or thirty of the names on my list for Dr. Contritus. I always include my name at the top of the list of substitutes because I am trying to be fair. I always give a false social security number, however, because my kind of fair just extends so far.

Dr. Contritus is the only person I was ever able to share every secret with, every small petty thing that I am, every miserable act I have committed, every cowardly deed, and every moment of joy and valor. There will be no one else the same for me, not ever. This I know.

I had a dog named Old Bob when I was a child. I shared everything with him, but he is long away.

He was a loving, all knowing being who was my shepherd when I was a child. So many years have passed and yet I miss him still as if only a day separated that now and then.

I had a cat I shared sadness with, but he never seemed to give a damn. He was a cantankerous, mean damn animal, who never loved me, but I loved him and I do not know why. I watched the cat die too and slept beside him on the floor so many nights until he left. I held him in my lap and wept.

> *I still miss that old stupid cat*
> *Who struggled so valiantly against the coming night*
> *Though he never loved me*

> *I still miss that old stupid cat*
> *Who accepted me for my food gathering*
> *And my attention to kitty litter*

> *I loved him so*
> *I loved his unbending will*
> *As he scraped his arthritic legs across the carpet*
> *To lay where the heat swam from the pipes*
> *In that last long winter*
> *And his determination to awaken me*
> *When cats must be fed*
> *On the new schedule his dying body demanded*

> *I still miss him so*
> *And if there is anything, anything of meaning*
> *He will again run swift and oh so sure*
> *Through hunting fields*

With vast herds of ground squirrels cavorting
And days full of mischief
And secret places from which to see and not be seen
And moonlight in which to dance
And swirling leaves to catch and tease

I loved him so
And he broke my heart
For his great courage
Weighted by so many long years
With pain ignored
And only cat dreams of yesterday's mischief revisited
To give solace in that last long winter
As he faded away into the sunlight on his windowsill
I still miss him so

Death is an excuse for maudlin, trite poems well felt and better left unshared. It is a time when all the sorrow for yourself can be expressed in praise of others; all the sadness of times past can fall in a river rushing through the mind and be revisited.

Having run its course, the river hesitates before falling into the sea, as if afraid of losing itself, but on in one last leap of faith it falls. Does it remember in the sea what it was to rush past meadows, and wander pathways along vast canyons stretching its long belly across the earth? Goodbye, old friend.

INSURANCE

Mr. Culswamp is inspecting the furniture in my office. He leaves a sneer on each piece of furniture and passes on. " Why can't I get out of here. You people just keep patients until their insurance runs out. Everybody knows that. I've got the best insurance, so I must stay in the damn place. I know if I leave against the judgement of my doctor, the insurance company won't pay. That is how you keep all these poor suckers in here."

"Let me ask you something. Why don't I hire you as a private psychologist and pay you directly? I could leave and you could get all the money for the treatment. I found out what your salary is and I know you could use the money. Look, you seem like a reasonable person, why not take my offer and make some money?" This is my second offer for the day. Numerous staff members have offered their meager checks if Mr. Culswamp can get a few days of electro-convulsive therapy.

"I presume that marvelously vacuous look means no. Forget it. This place is the intellectual pits, the underarm of intelligence. What? You think there is some deep Freudian horror in my past that makes me have a few drinks from time to time. I've read Freud." At this point Dr. Freud enters the room, sits on the uncomfortable red chair and shoots up a seven percent solution. I ask for a connection, but he nods wisely and states, "It is not meaningful unless you pay for it."

"You think it has something to do with my childhood. You think it's probably about my father. That is ridiculous because I worshiped my father. He knew more than anyone I know." Mr. Culswamp inspects the alter of his gold Rolex watch with acolytes of diamonds at its call. "What do you remember of your mother, Mr. Culswamp?" I ask in ambush by his road.

"I remember the boring witch left us when I was twelve years old. I remember that quite distinctly. Is that a Freudian possibility? Sure I remember her. What, you don't remember people that screwed you?

She left us, my father and me, but we didn't need her anyway. She was not worthy of my father. Her family came from some place in Georgia. Maybe they were sharecroppers for all I know. They were dirt poor and they never came to New York, not even for a visit and we never visited them. Well, I guess she visited them sometimes, but we never went. She did not understand what the good things in life are about. She was always arguing with my father about things he was doing, business things that were none of her business."

"Do you remember what she was like?"

"She was a short brunette. She smelled nice. I don't really remember. She was good to me, I guess. I know he hit her once before she left, but she was in his face about something she thought was unethical. You wouldn't understand, but that does not have anything to do with what my father was talking about. He was talking about a business deal, not a social gathering. She used to take me to the zoo and the museums a lot. She read to me all the time when I was a child . . . but it was just crap, it didn't have anything to do with real life."

"Do you remember why she left?"

"She is just a woman. Who knows why they do things, such silly things. I really do not know. She just left. I guess she would say it was because my father was unethical and cheated people, but he said she just left. I know he hit her that once, but for good reason. He was never violent with anyone. He was a good man. He was hard about some things, but he was a good man. It was easier to talk with her, but she was a woman and it didn't really matter."

"Did she ever try to contact you before she died?"

"I don't know. I mean, her sister said she tried all the time and she missed me terribly, but I never got a call or a letter. Her sister says my father wouldn't let her see me or call me, but I don't know if that is true. It seems she could have found me if she wanted to. I know she came to the house a few times and he wouldn't let her in, but he was trying to protect us."

"How did you feel when she committed suicide?"

Mr. Culswamp looks at his mother sitting in the red chair with her white dress. She looks up from her book and smiles, a quiet encompassing smile that touches the side of Mr. Culswamp's cheek and lingers for a moment. "He said she was weak. He said she did it to makes us feel guilty when it was all her fault to begin with. I don't remember how I felt. It was a long time ago. She would probably have liked this tawdry little berg we are living in now. She liked the most stupid things. She did not know the value of money and how hard it is to make. She really liked the most stupid things. I don't really remember how I felt." Freud nods wisely in his chair as the seven percent solution solves the riddle within the lotus.

REAL NUMBERS

Today is indeed momentous. Dr. Mondriatus has taken me to meet Dr. Bruno. Dr. Bruno works in the sub-x level of the hospital. No one knows how deep underground the sub-x level reaches. One hears stories.

The sub-x level houses the lab where many experiments take place. Dr. Bruno uses dogs for his experiments. The dogs are all pedigreed labrador retrievers. Dr. Bruno does not have any humans to experiment on because he was born too late. Dr. Bruno is a large man who wears three white lab coats, one on top of the other. All of the lab coats have his name and degrees. Dr. Mondriatus has disappeared into a small alcove lit by incense candles.

I am alone with Dr. Bruno. This is not a good feeling. Dr. Bruno has the look about him of those who deal with death on a daily basis, not those who work to save lives and see death in the process, but those who can pass out death at will. Such beings carry about them the aurora of those who have stepped beyond their own being into the realm of the gods. Like some ancient priest, robed in darkness, and standing at the top of a tall stone pyramid, Dr. Bruno sees us all from a great distance. Yet, Dr. Bruno also gives the impression of being a simple journeyman performing what is demanded and asking no more than to do his job well.

Dr. Bruno was once a professional hockey player before an injury forced him to make a living as a physiologist. Dr. Bruno still wants to be a hockey player. His body knows this and has developed a uniform of ectoplasm. His number is difficult to read, but the dude would high-stick you in a New York instant.

The lab is full of threatening smells. The smells follow you wherever you go. There are endless rows of cages with numbers on them. In the cages are hundreds of dogs. Some of the dogs bark and try to make friends. They send the staff birthday cards and Christmas cards, all to no avail.

Most of the dogs have tubes that run into their bodies. Some have the noise of death about them. There are those resigned to their fate, their eyes betray no thoughts of hope beyond a quick end to life. Some dogs do not understand their fate and continue to try to communicate with the humans they believe will help them. Their genetic pool has trapped them.

"This is number 682. We are testing the effects of various levels of alcohol ingestion on the function of the cardiovascular system," states Dr. Bruno as he lights up a Marlboro. Number 682 has eyes of no-place-left-to-go. Number 682 and I avoid eye contact.

"Jesus, I can see the look on your face. Don't give me the bird's breath crap about harming defenseless animals. You would want the information, if it would save your life. That's what this is all about and that's why someone has to do it. You want the solutions without the pain it takes to get them. It hurts me as much as it hurts you, but someone has to do it if we are going to make any headway in helping the people that need help. I'm not doing this to get my name on any more journal articles. I've got about 50,000 right now. Get any sanctimonious crap out of your mind and don't come down here anymore. You never even played hockey. I used to play hockey. At least number 682 has a number and a meaning," states Dr. Bruno as he looks at his lab coats for a number.

Actually, you do not know what I am thinking, Dr. Bruno. I am thinking I should kill you and all your staff, all the poor, sad bastards that work in this vile place. But, I do not just wish to kill you, I want to rip your guts out and hear you scream. I am ashamed by the fact that I would enjoy hearing you scream. I would revel in the possibility. I know that after the madness had gone, I would be horrified by what I had done, but I know I would be joyous in the moment with my hands deep into the blood of your being.

I hate for more reasons than the horrifying pain these beings are receiving each moment of their existence. I hate because of all the moments I have felt helpless against some powerful being who held me captive and in pain. I hate for all of us who are faced with beings and circumstances that leave us pinned within our cages, ranting against a foe we cannot comprehend or defeat.

I want to kill every damn thing in this place, and most of all I want to kill myself for having experienced the possibility and being a coward and taking no action, and probably being willing to let one of these dogs die to save my life. But I do not believe I would ask the dog, even if I was dying, but I do not know, I do not know and this is saddest of all. How can this crap go on and on, never ending horrors of action and omission?

THE THREE-HEADED GOD

There are moans in the night in the parking lot of the Eumolpidae Bar and Grill. The night moans for me and the lovely lady by my side. No. The moans are coming from the passenger side of a Mustang bathed in a cascade of electric light. The lady insists we investigate. Jesus.

Beside the car Dr. Grantus is kneeling with his head on the ground. He is not facing Mecca unless they have moved it. Wait, in the beginning Muhammad directed them towards Jerusalem. Possibly Dr. Grantus is of the old school. "Help him. He really looks in a bad way," says the lady of the night. "Nonsense, Dr. Grantus is an extremely devout man and is simply saying his evening prayers." "Is this not so, Dr. Grantus?"

"I'm going to kill you if I ever get up from here, you bastard." This will undoubtedly detract from the efficacy of Dr. Grantus' request to his maker. Or possibly not.

"Alas, most beautiful of ladies, I must, with great reluctance, aid my brother in his prayers and send you back into the night from whence you came. Go, and know that I lust for you in dark corners of quiet places and that your name shall be in both of our prayers this night and every night that falls upon us."

"You're both fruitcakes. Are you going to be here tomorrow night?" Now there is a question indeed. Shall we be here tomorrow night? Shall we be anywhere tomorrow night? Is this moment lived forever? Is time a series of infinite loops between an infinite number of dimensions? We are both fruitcakes for sure. Dr. Grantus is the head of the new alcoholism prevention program at the hospital. Obviously he is engaged in a momentous research project.

His present position is the result of the three-headed god. Anu, Enlil and Enki have proven too much for Dr. Grantus, or, just enough, as the case may be. We have spent the afternoon and well into this good night at the Eumolpidae Bar and Grill. On Thursdays, a day scared to the god Anu, all drinks are three-for-one. Both a religious and economic imperative prevail on such a day.

Dr. Grantus has been drinking double tequila sunrises all night. The table was bathed in a warm glow and the sound of the surf flowing softly on the beach could be heard from a great distance. Around midnight, Dr. Grantus added to the effect by urinating from the second floor balcony onto the packed herd of patrons beneath. It is to be admired that no one seemed to mind the yellow rain; many in fact remarked favorably on the idea of having the premises misted at the stroke of midnight.

At some point during the night Enlil took over Dr. Grantus' persona and became somewhat belligerent. On three occasions he offered to beat the shit out of the cocktail waitress. He also sent threatening notes to two people in wheelchairs, but the notes were somewhat unintelligible and we received a free round of drinks. Dr. Grantus remembered only later that one of the lads in a wheelchair was a former patient. At this point he became irrate that a patient would be out drinking after the work that Dr. Grantus had put into curing him. He immediately set off to attack the ungrateful wretch, but he had already wheeled himself out of the place to the relative safety of the night carrying the heavy burden of his ingratitude for Dr. Grantus' devoted service to him. Does no one appreciate the work we do?

I am sitting next to Dr. Grantus in the parking lot of the Eumolpidae Bar and Grill. Only two cars remain in the parking lot. For once, I will be able to find my car with relative ease. A soft rain is beginning to fall. Dr. Grantus continues to pray. I will stay next to Dr. Grantus until we are both able to continue our appointed rounds and the gods have left for new and more promising acquisitions.

The Weeds of God

EVEN THERAPISTS GET THE BLUES

What in the world is this all about? Everybody is depressed, frightened and lost. That is what I can see from here. I have been other places and seen it differently. I think this one is the right one, or one of the right ones, however.

Does no one have a good childhood? What a horror the damn thing is, this time of smallness enunciated. You are at the mercy of all who surround you. Are there no parents that can overcome their own small fears?

Every therapist should have to take philosophy, anthropology, and sociology. Let us all bask in the magnificence of chaos. What does all this crap mean? No one is what they appear. Everyone, including me, projects an image onto the screen of life that they believe best protects and endears. Plato stands behind each of us with a projector. The only ones left without a shadow are the sociopaths.

I understand my patients because I am them. It is all a matter of degrees. I know that everyone is scared and easily hurt by the words and deeds of others. I know that they try desperately to cover up the hurt they feel. I know I am scared every day of my life and so are they. I know I seek excitement and peace. I know there are multiple competing drive states that cause havoc, and make terror of decisions. I know I too feel like changing my state of mind with a plethora of pharmacological possibilities. I maintain only because of genetic inheritance and specific, accidental experiential realities. I seek to rearrange how my patients view past experiences, and to change their perception of present experiences, and improve possible responses to present problem situations. Jesus, it all seems so damn hopeless. I must look for more possibilities. *Lacrimae rerum.*

"Did you like my *Dispatches from Gaul*?" asks Caesar. I loved them as a matter of fact. Brilliantly written and great reading. I love to read about war. I like to know how it ends before I read it, however. There is such comfort in the finality of it. "You are experiencing an anxiety of leadership. Leading is its own reason for being. Some of you wishes to sleep, but part of you, the greater part, wants to lead in times of crisis, to give the orders that set victory in motion."

Why did you do the corrupt things you did? I know you were a great man, a valorous man, a man of loyalty, a man of great intellect and insight into yourself and your fellow beings. Why? "What you describe as corrupt was for me the time in which I lived. Did not Jefferson own slaves? You cannot judge me out of the context in which I existed, just as you cannot judge yourself except in relation to some fixed context of being. Is this not true?" I do not know. I am not sure who is making the judgements that appear in my mind. How can I be making a judgement on myself? Who the hell is judging whom? If atoms are not alive and people are composed of atoms, then how are people alive? "Why ask a question that has no answer. Why not concentrate on those questions for which you may find a suitable answer. You will find no one truth, no matter how hard you try. You seek a certainty that life cannot provide unless you simply make it up as most of us do. Is that not what you do? Do you not help others to create a reality, a certainty in which they can abide with some acceptable degree of security and happiness?" Yes, that is what I do. It seems the only way to give them an escape from the pain they feel. I help them to rearrange the building blocks of their existence to construct a place in which they can safely exist. I know this, but I also know that it is all a construction. Where is the reality. I say to myself that this is the only reality, but is this the truth? "Is it not the case that each truth exists to provide the best explanation for all the voices that speak in our mind until a better truth comes along. What else do you suggest there is of truth? *Quantum sufficit.*"

THE SEPOY REBELLION

He is such a gracious man, Dr. Bobriatus. He is willing to share all his accomplishments with his fellow beings. His servant Sing Cantbe follows him into the room shining a large flashlight on his master's large diamond ring.

"I would have discharged me long ago. There is really nothing left to discuss. I was temporarily impaired due to an incredible amount of stress in dealing with my patients and I momentarily self-medicated with alcohol. That, I believe, sums up the situation completely. There is no further need for intervention. The stress is now perfectly under control and I am prepared to resume my practice. It is ridiculous for you, someone without even the semblance of my credentials and training, to pass judgement on me. I would of course leave now, but my lawyer has advised me that I need to follow all the appropriate procedures. I am getting very tired of putting up with your lack of respect and your obvious desire to punish your betters. Dr. Mondriatus has been ascertained of my feelings on this matter and wholeheartedly concurs. He explained that he would be handling the case, but he wished to avoid any semblance of preferential treatment for someone like me. You will be removed as a therapist from my case unless you are willing to be reasonable," states Dr. Bobriatus and lights up a Newport with his gold Dunhill. Sing is in the corner with the other Sepoys discussing the use of pig fat to lubricate cartridges. I nod at them as Sing screams, "May the infidels feel the wrath of Allah. *Jihad*."

"Possibly you have been influenced by my wife's conversation. Incidentally, I did not give my permission for you to intrude into my personal life by having a session with my wife, but I can assure you that whatever information she gave you is tainted by the fact that she is filing for divorce and seeking every asset I possess. If you discuss my problems with her, I can assure you that it will not only be a matter of ethics, but a civil procedure that will empty your meager pockets of all they possess. The woman is sick. She has had numerous affairs with the most shabby individuals. Contrary to what she has told you, I have always acted in an ethical manner in relation to my patients. What exactly did she tell you?"

"Does writing prescriptions for morphine for patients and using them yourself ring a bell?" We will wait till they sleep tonight and fall upon them, my brothers. *Jihad.*

"I knew it. That worthless bitch. She will do anything to vilify me. There is no way to prove such an accusation. I have never, never betrayed my sacred oath. I truly feel that I am virtually one with Aesculapius. If you chart this or say anything about it, I will ruin you no matter what it takes." Dr. Brobiatus has turned a lovely shade of red. I believe it is the pig fat, my brothers. Aesculapius has entered the room and is talking with Sing and the rest of the Sepoys. He is holding one of the hated cartridges and pointing to Dr. Brobiatus. In actuality, the lovely Mrs. Dr. Bobriatus said nothing about morphine, but she has accepted Allah as the one true God and is planning to participate in the rebellion. *Inshallah.*

SOMEDAY THIS WAR WILL END

The road stretches into the distance, the dirt brown tail of some great snake that waits. In the treeline the Hated-Cong are reading Grimm's Fairy Tales and eating chop-chop. Mr. Hamsung's dog tag is in his boot.

"I've been dreaming about the war again. I don't dream of bad times. The times seem pleasant and familiar, like young puppies that cuddle to my warmth. I wonder why they keep coming back? Maybe it is all I really have. My wife still hasn't called. The number at the house has been changed. I wrote her a long letter yesterday. If only she would give me one more chance, I won't screw it up again. Do you think she will give me another go?" Mr. Hamsung looks at his therapist who is not brave enough to say that there is a letter in the mail. I must tell him, but not today, not today. Each day I think I will be able to talk her into one more try, but I can see the distance widening as the road stretches into the future.

The Hated-Cong are firing RPG's with American newspapers for projectiles. They are deadly, the most deadly of all. "Maybe I should tell her how I really feel. Christ! I don't know what I would really tell her. I'm confused about everything. Nothing seems to have any meaning except keeping her. She is all I have left. I think about her all the time. I know, why wasn't I thinking about her when I went on the windmill? In a way I was. I feel I can't give her what she wants. I don't seem to be able to give anyone what they want. My mother doesn't tell anyone I was in the Marines anymore. She used to be so proud. Now she acts like it never happened. It's like she believes I have done something wrong that we should all hide. Nothing seems to end the damn war. Some of me wants it to go on forever and some of me wants it over; just get the damn thing over." The Hated-Cong bow their heads. They shall miss it too.

ON THE LISP OF DIAGNOSTICS

Dr. Argetto has found a new diagnosis, post traumatic stress disorder (PTSD). Last month it was Tourettes. I think his new one is a great step in the right direction. I do, however, disagree with almost all of his diagnostic possibilities.

Dr. Argetto weighs in around three hundred pounds and gets all his suits from a place on Main Street that specializes in recycling clothing from deceased vagrants. You sew a couple of them together and *Voila!* He is an amazing fellow who is well read in the classics and flies his own four-seater Cessna. When he gets in this puppy, it looks like someone stuck a large turnip in a matchbox.

Dr. Argetto's diagnostic abilities are suspect at best. He is the only psychiatrist I know who is more of an interior decorator for mental disorders. I say, this year we simply cannot have any paranoids. They are out, totally out, old thing. We speak of post traumatic stress disorder, and some blood red drapes for the psyche. This mind screams for post traumatic stress disorder.

Dr. Argetto also has a marvelously lovely lisp which he has cultivated over the years. He went to Cambridge. This explains many things.

Dr. Argetto has asked me to sit in on his discussion with the family of a patient he is treating. For reasons known only to Dr. Argetto, he believes I am an expert in post traumatic stress disorder. This may be because I have argued with him about diagnosing every veteran who has the misfortune to come to us as PTSD.

PTSD has become very popular with veterans since they can pick up some meaningful disability benefits if they can find Dr. Argetto. Veterans can apparently have this disorder even though they never saw a day of combat. It is, after all, the thought that counts.

Mr. Hernendez is Dr. Argetto's latest discovery. He served in Vietnam as a cook in DaNang. Apparently the food was worse than everyone thought. Mr. Hernendez's parents are first generation Mexican-Americans and they seem quite amazed by the whole prospect that public drunkenness can have such bizarre consequences in America. Mr. Hernendez got in a fight with some policeman who brought him here for detoxification. Apparently hitting him on the head with their night-sticks did not produce the desired results. Having Mr. Hernendez assigned to Dr. Argetto was just another stroke of good fortune for the lad.

Mr. Hernendez's father is well dressed and speaks English relatively well, at least as well as most of the staff. Mr. Hernendez's mother does not speak English quite as well, and is wearing an outfit that would make a gypsy weep. Dr. Argetto looks enviously at the many contrasting colors.

"Ples be assurhed that we are doing everything for you sohn," states Dr. Argetto. Mr. Hernendez's father is obviously revisiting his Berlitz course pronunciations and looks questioningly at me. I, of course, produce one of my more reassuring smiles and tap the side of my head twice. "It is my opinion that your sohn is suffering fram post traumatic dress disorder." At this point Mr. Hernendez's father looks at Mr. Hernendez's mother and the marvelous rainbow of colors in which she is entwined. "This occurers when someone is subzected to dress that is simply too much to bare." Mr. Hernendez's mother begins to look at her dress. Mr. Hernendez's father simply looks confused. "May I add tha your sohn is also entitled to compensation from the government for wah he has suffered." Mr. Hernendez's father appears now quite bewildered indeed. I mean, it's bad, but an emotional disorder? Only in America. And, you can get money for it too? Madre de Dios, this is a wonderful country.

Yes, that is correct. The whole thing can be explained quite rationally when you look at past dresses that Mr. Hernendez's mother has worn over the course of some twenty years. Presuming that what she has on today is in the relatively subdued range, Mr. Hernendez has had twenty years of visual experiences that would throw terror in to the souls of lesser men.

Soon we will demand a scrapbook of all the pictures of dresses worn by Mr. Hernendez's mother. The clinical team will peruse these babies and develop an individual treatment plan to help Mr. Hernendez work through all his past traumatic dress encounters. I love this place.

LARKS AND TOMATOES

The sky is worn and threadbare today. It is an old sky just reshuffled from a pile of old skies and dealt without intent to defraud. I do not mind.

Mr. Coggins is happy today because he loves old worn skies that have been dealt out for the millionth time. He likes everything old and worn. Mr. Coggins has been having bouts with alcoholism for the past fifty years. Mr. Coggins is the Joe Foreman of alcoholism. He has won over and over, but that old demon rum just picks himself up and demands a rematch, and Mr. Coggins always gives it to him because Mr. Coggins is that way.

"I went seven months this time. I thought I had him licked. Seven months, that's a long time, seven months. It was the tomatoes. I love a beer with real summer tomatoes. That's how it started. I really love tomatoes. I remember the smell of the garden when I was a child, the smell of dirt and ripening tomatoes. It's a wonderful smell, it's summer." There are people picking tomatoes in the garden down below. They are wearing sun bonnets and smiles. I watch them meandering between the endless rows of tomatoes and the sun that lays with quilted shadows across the field.

Mr. Coggins is such a good man. He has no friends and he has nothing to do because he has no farm on which to care for his tomatoes. Mr. Coggins is very lonely. Mr. Coggins is very dull in a sweet, competent fashion. There has never been a woman in Mr. Coggins' life. He is shy and unable to speak in their presence. He does not lie or cheat or bear false witness against his neighbors. Mr. Coggins will never find that farm again where the tomatoes grow row on row with the larks still bravely singing in the sky.

BEOWULF'S BITCH

There is a breeze trickling down from the air-conditioner. It smells like piles of rusted steel.

"My sister had a large mole on her left breast," states Mr. James. "I have seen it on the surface of the moon, the same mole indeed, indeed. How many times must a cannonball fly before it rests in the sand? We were just a single person looking for a hole in a door. I miss that. It will never rest in the sand, old friend. There are those on this unit who have done murderous things which I have not in my wildest dreams. Why can't you make love to your sister? Why? It is some silly Biblical crap that is meaningless. It has nothing to do with people's feelings towards one another. Who does it harm, pray tell, dear Yorick? No one, it harms no one, but the beast. We defeated the beast, but he lives forever where the cannonball lands." The crown of upper and lower Egypt rests on the table. The sand brushes against it and falls at its master's feet.

Mr. James stands up and begins to pace back and forth. The Nubian slaves follow fanning him with great ostrich plumes. He is deciding wether to launch his great army past the fourth cataract into the desert of time.

"Do you remember much about your father?"

"A marvelously stupid question. I do not have to remember for you are my father and still the sly old fox. I have hidden more from you than you will know. Sly. The whole thing is very sly. I need another blanket for my room. We should have blankets. The armies of the insane should have blankets to wear against the cold. I do not like my medication. It makes me slow to recall. Sometimes I do not even remember what it is I should recall. I know I would recall my life. Is there a redial button for life? Punch that bitch and let's be on our way. Have you read *The Painted Bird*? She is my painted bird. She is the bird of paradise. She is gone. Shit on her and die. I would kill a thousand fold that which harmed us. In a thousand nights, I would slay the beast a thousand times. I feel remorse for Beowulf and the bitch he slew. I feel remorse for morning too. I feel remorse for me and you, for we are the weeds of God. Not you. Not you." The sand shapes itself around his feet and remembers the sea.

SINGLE CELLED LOBACHEVKIAN ORGANISMS

"I speak to you of the single celled orgasm. That's my proposition for this day of life. What is it about evolution that leaves us high and dry on this vast ocean of space? How did all this emerge from some amino acids? I think I've got you on this one. Think. Amino acids and electromagnetic energy cannot be the answer." Mr. James begins to burn his first edition of *On the Origin of Species,* one page at a time in the ashtray.

"Where did we begin? How did we begin? Do you think upon this? I am the beginning of many things. Many things have begun with me. I will end with me. There will be no more I. I am space, and water mostly. What makes me think these thoughts I think? How does it occur? I have never seen a real explanation that does not beg another and another to eternity. I am looking into the species of origin. That is the place to look." The ship is fragile upon the dark, blue sea and floats toward a destiny of origins.

I talked with Mr. James' sister on the phone the other day. She had a melodic, caressing voice. She did not wish her brother to know where she lived or her married name. I asked her if she could possibly come to Memphis for some sessions with her brother and she said, "He has told you?" Before I could respond, my momentary silence had spoken and the line went dead. The ship is fragile upon the dark, blue sea and a destiny of origins is abandoned. No single wave holds meaning. Is there a meaning that could be dissected from some greater part of the whole? We are a single linear cell within a Lobachevskian geometry which denies Mr. James' existence.

THE LADY-WHO-WAS-WITH-ME

The light of the candle bends with the wind and leaps back to begin again. I am on the balcony of a high-rise apartment building that cannot forget it was once a department store. Somewhere inside the apartment a woman sleeps who is unaware I am still alive. It is two o'clock in the morning of tomorrow and a hard rain is falling, demanding thunder and lightening at will from the sky. The flame of the candle is untroubled by the thunder and lightening, only fearing the wind shark. I am lonely, but I do not wish to begin again. I sip the Grey Goose and remember when.

I have betrayed again; not by a clause in any contract, but in the knowledge that I would give pain. Now I cannot fathom the choice because the sexual drive state has been satiated and is empty of demands.

She was so beautiful, slim with large eyes and perfect features. She wanted to listen to my words. I wanted someone new who could be delighted by the magic of stories told before.

The lady-who-was-with-me left within a pique as I knew she would. I paid too much attention to an otherwise. The lady-who-was-with-me left and I played out the hand the night had dealt. I am so desperately sad of what I have done. The lady-who-was-with-me would stand beside you when all others were lost to their own fears. I have known her a long time, the lady-who-was-with-me, and this I know.

The woman-for-the-night I had not known, and this, and her beauty, drew me to her. It was an evolutionary mandate, an evolutionary mandate I had the opportunity to overcome and failed. I am weak for such things, but I am beginning to remember. So much of wisdom is a sound memory of our own mistakes. If only I could remember these little aphorisms when such possibilities appear.

The woman-for-the-night was momentarily enthralled. Old, and much used, magic sufficed beyond reason, and I was without all the small, and large, imperfections known to the lady-who-was-with-me.

I will not be here for the woman-for-the-night when she awakes although I promised I would be, and I believe she would like it so, if only to make it seem important in a passing way. But, I will not be here for the woman-for-the-night when she awakes. I am a coward for such things.

I have been emptied of the need although I know it will fall upon me again. I have no time now for the possibility, and no time has me. But, the lady-who-was-with-me, she has me. It is her time with me that binds, and it is the lack of time with the woman-for-the-night that drew me momentarily to her. Sad, so sad, is it not? I was full of drink and full of myself, and I betrayed, giving needless pain.

Had I been sober, or just had sex, I might have been immune to my own betrayal. There is, alas, no truth in drink; but, come to think of it, that is why it is so alluring. Truth demands and drink excuses. Why do I seek so many possibilities of being excused?

LARGE DOGS AND ROADS IN TIME

I hear the sound of myriad commodes flushing and in comes Mr. Culswamp. He trips lightly over the small hole in the rug and looks at me in disgust. I must remember to put a bear trap in that baby when I get a chance.

"I thought about what you said about my father. Maybe he was too hard on my mother, but she left us. I mean, when you get down to it, she left us. He didn't leave. He stayed and took care of me. He must have been hurt a lot, but he never said a word. He never said anything about any pain he felt. I know he was sad. Well, I guess he was sad. Sometimes it was hard to tell. She left us, that's the real issue. She left us." Mr. Culswamp stands in the dusk at the back door, looking at his mother growing smaller and smaller as she vanishes into the road that runs through his mind. He is very small, Mr. Culswamp, and very much alone.

"I always wanted a dog when I was a child. She wanted to get one, but father explained that they were messy and useless. I've never had a dog. I won't let my wife get one. He was right about dogs. I guess he was right about almost everything. Maybe he should not have hit her. She was meddling where she didn't belong, but maybe he should not have hit her. I didn't hit her." Mr. Culswamp is yelling to his mother down the back road of his mind that he did not hit her. But then, he has paid her back in his own desperate way.

"You're right, I do think about her sometimes. I think what it would have been like to grow up with her there. It would have been different. I guess it would have been different. Maybe it wouldn't have been any better. I don't know. Maybe it would have been a softer time. It wasn't his fault though. It was just as much, or more, her fault. When you think about it, you can see what his point was." Mr. Culswamp turns from the road and the shape that vanishes in the distance to the large, empty figure who holds him in the shadows.

"Maybe he hit her more than one time. Maybe there were some other times he hit her. I really don't know. It's true, I don't know. Sometimes I think I remember other times and sometimes I don't. I really don't remember, but I remember she left and she never came back." Mr. Culswamp's mother is back standing in the road, looking at him in the doorway of time. She has on the same dress that his father said was cheap. She has the same smell. She has the same foolish smile.

"Then she left us twice. Jesus, once wasn't enough. She left us twice. She put a bullet through her head and left us again. He was hurt, but he never said anything. He was a man. He wasn't maudlin or silly about it. He said it was because she wanted to hurt us. I guess he was right. She must have been very lonely too. I guess she was very lonely, just like me. She must have been so alone." Mrs. Culswamp walks over and touches him on the arm, just the slightest of touches. She turns and walks back down the road and beside her there is a large black and white dog that skips at her heels.

The Weeds of God

THE LAST SQUIRREL

There is a large white squirrel sitting on my windowsill and starring at Mr. Thanaten. Mr. Thanaten has attempted suicide on two occasions. He may have succeeded on one of these occasions. I do not know.

"I was sitting in the car, my Jaguar that never runs but looks lovely parked in front of the house. It was late at night and a dark rain was falling. I put the .38 snub-nose to the left side of my head and pulled the trigger. I went somewhere and then I came back to where I was when I pulled the trigger. I remember the smell of cordite and the sound of rain on the roof. I love the sound of rain on the roof." Mr. Thanaten lights another cigarette and watches the rain blowing against the window pane.

"I remember pulling the trigger. Quite distinctly, I remember pulling the trigger. There was no hole in the passenger side window. There should have been a hole there. There was no hole anywhere in the car. There was no hole in my head. There was only the smell of cordite and the sound of rain falling on the roof. I like the smell of cordite. Maybe I am with Ambrose Bierce falling towards the water from the bridge, so far below the water and so long the fall. Maybe I have found a door into another dimension. Maybe Jaguars actually run in this dimension." Mr. Thanaten watches the smoke rise from his cigarette and looks for holes in the neighborhood.

"I remember that I did not want to pull the trigger again. The gun lay beneath the dashboard. I had wanted to use it as a passport to the other side, whatever that might be. I do not remember what I sought, only that what I had known had become increasingly uncomfortable with sudden, stunning flashes of depression. Even the strongest are hit by startling jabs of humiliation, and the weak are always standing in the middle of a freeway of speeding instances of random degradation. Yet, there are moments of frightening joy. Maybe these are spacers for the other so that we may better appreciate their impact." Mr. Thanaten avoids eye contact and there is mild psychomotor agitation present.

"Cordite, yes I remember the smell of cordite. When I was a child, I used to shoot an old Remington .22 bolt-action rifle. I would shoot a couple of hundred rounds every day. We lived on a large farm and the nearest neighbor was five miles away. The rifle was taller than I was. I would shoot all day long. I killed so many things that I cannot remember. So many. Birds, bullfrogs, squirrels, and rabbits fell before my hand. I was an incredibly good shot. It was all I did all day long. I did not know the pain they knew. I simply did not know. Then one day I shot a squirrel from the highest tree in the forest. When he fell to the ground, I picked him up, and, not knowing that he was dead, he bit into my thumb and looked into my eyes. I still have the scar and the remembrance of his terror and pain transfused into my veins. I will never hunt again. His horror and fear flow within my memory. We are one within the river, but only I am in this place and this now, and here I will not forget. Whatever river that now flows through him is part of me also and forever." Mr. Thanaten looks through me at the dream in which he lives. I am just part of Mr. Thanaten's dream. We are all just part of Mr. Thanaten's dream. This is quite comforting. I will sleep well with the sound of the rain on the roof and the smell of cordite.

The Weeds of God

CONGRESSMAN BUNDNUT'S THREE POINT PEN

The great examiners are on the horizon, the Joint Commission on Accreditation of Healthcare Organizations (JCAHO). In three weeks they will arrive with palm leaves laid as a carpet unto their feet. This place is absolute bedlam. I just love it.

JCAHO means life or death for the hospital. Without JCAHO accreditation, no medicaid patients can be billed. There is much more to it, however. Not receiving JCAHO accreditation is the kiss of death for the hospital administration. It means we are not good at what we do, or, in reality, that we are not good at faking documentation that indicates we are good at doing what we are supposed to be doing. For every thirty minutes of service delivered to the patient, it takes about twenty minutes to document the service in all the right locations in the patient's chart.

Every year there is something new in the survey so that you cannot get a real standard operating procedure that will be successful every time. This year we have cardinal events and new restraint procedures.

Cardinal events are something that drastically effects the patient's well being. We must document these and our corrective action plan for any instance of a cardinal event. Cardinal events occur in this place on a daily basis. Just having Dr. Lambast as your therapist should be listed as a cardinal event.

Restraint procedures have been taken to a new high of madness due to congressional hearings on the abuses involved in restraint procedures. Former patients have testified before Congress that they were abused on a regular basis during restraint procedures and barely had time to recuperate before they were abducted by aliens. Congressmen are certain that being against abuse is supported by a large percentage of the voting population and, as a result, they solidly support changing all the regulations to ensure the whole thing is a farce.

We now have to check the patient every five minutes during the restraint procedure to insure all their vital signs indicate they are experiencing no discomfort. This is supposed to be done while we are wrestling the little charmers on the floor as they hit, spit, scratch, bite and generally attempt to give bodily harm to their beloved mental health workers. Seems damn reasonable to me. Please remove your hands from my throat long enough for me to check your pulse, Mr. Caligula.

It was interesting to note that during these congressional hearings, the senators and congressmen demanded triple the usual security guards in their chambers. Let them wrestle a few of those giving testimony for fifteen minutes or so, and I will have more faith in the hearings. Congressman Bundnut is on him like greased lighting! Applying a sanctioned upper body hold, the congressman takes him to the mat, quickly checks his pulse, and whether he is registered to vote in his district. Finding no registration, Congressman Bundnut immediately applies more pressure and goes for a three point pen. There is a round of applause for Congressman Bundnut before he is awarded the heavyweight belt and a lifetime supply of Haldol.

Abuse does occur, but so do car accidents. Do we get rid of the cars to stop all the accidents or do we sanction those who cause the accidents? This is an amazing country. We constantly go from one extreme to the other. Is there no place for logic and a reasonable approach to the issues? Mr. Caligula is sneaking up behind Congressman Bundnut as he holds his belt up for the audience to admire. Mr. Caligula is holding a folding chair.

When patients become violent they need to be restrained to prevent physical harm to themselves, other patients and staff. After all, there is no indication that becoming a mental health worker abrogates all your rights to be protected against those who would do you bodily harm. Numerous legislators immediately begin to look through federal law for indications this may be true.

Any mental health worker who deliberately harms a patient should be prosecuted under the law. Seems reasonable. To give harm to those who cannot fight back, or those who are impaired by mental illness, is a heinous act. To say that the patient has the right to attack others with impunity, however, is ridiculous. They must be stopped from injuring self or others, and sometimes only restraints can prevent the possibility. There is a time when de-escalation procedures just do not work well. When Mr. Caligula has Mr. Edwards on the floor and is beating the hell out of him, de-escalation leaves a little to be desired. Now, if it was Congressman Bundnut, I would take ten or fifteen minutes to try to talk Mr. Caligula out of killing the congressman. I might even invest more time in such an attempt. I would even be willing to take Mr. Caligula's vital signs to be sure that killing the congressman is not causing undue physical strain on Mr. Caligula.

JCAHO seems to be the essence of the new world order. It is more important to appear to be doing right than it is to be doing right. Soon I will go next door to the bar and discuss all this with my colleagues knowing that there will be no rational changes made within this never ending process. I love this place.

TIME DISSECTED

Why is there so much pain in growing up? I begin to believe that no one can be a good parent. Even good parents must inevitably give pain.

"You trouble yourself with questions that are meaningless. Do you take enjoyment from battle with your own uncertainty?"

I am not sure what I take enjoyment from anymore, dear Caesar. I seem to question everything too much. I not only look gift horses in the mouth, I run a CAT scan on them.

"Take what is given to you and act upon it. There is always sadness and despair for those who seek it."

And you too, Caesar? Is there no explanation for the terrifying unfairness of the world? I see all these people chained to the heartaches of their past and inflicting heartache on themselves and others in now and future times. I see people preyed upon by others and destroyed. I see a vomit of meanness all about me. I see politicians, lawyers and media pogues raping themselves and us each day. It stinks and I am ready to depart.

"Your are wallowing in a bed of sorrow. You fluff it up about you, a nest for your own imagined righteousness. It helps neither you, nor those you serve. Wake up King Arthur. Camelot must have rats and vermin for eagles do not feed on milk and honeydew. Be happy there are endless battles left to fight, and breath and steel left to fight them with. Look in wonder upon this field of battle. Feel the river of lightning that runs through you and the those who stand with you. Feel the sun upon you this last day upon the earth. Know that you will fight always this battle, with the sun just this size within the heavens, the smell of the earth that will claim you, the presence of the others who stand with you, and the granite resolve to stay until the end. This is all there is. Few will know it even once within their lives, or only for a fleeting moment they will forever seek again. Do not make it tawdry by dissecting it, for everything is small, so very small, when magnified to minutiae."

VOICES IN THE RAIN

Mr. Quimpers looks out the window into the rain that falls on the Taj Mahal. His head is cocked as if listening to some small sound falling from the rain. His left foot jerks in a chaos of partial rhythms once remembered. "I remember words of prey. They fall upon me like eagles ripping red from my still beating heart. I am hemorrhaging my past."

Alexandros speaks, "My father was not as great as I. He held Greece to his will, but I held all the world to mine." Mr. Quimpers looks at Alexandros, then turns to listen for the voices in the rain.

"I loved once. I loved deeply. I loved even honor, and maybe honor more. Maybe I loved honor so much because I thought it made me greater than I am, to love that which has no extension other than the momentary synapse. Maybe I thought it small to love things with only carbon based life. I forget. No, I have never known. I did not look until they had taken all else from me. And when I looked, when I looked, it had slipped away." Mr. Quimpers traces the initials "CQ" in the rain frost upon the window. Charlene Quimpers.

"I loved her so. I am not a romantic man. No, I am a romantic man, but I do not know how to please a woman well. I tried very hard, but I do not know how to please a woman well. I was away a lot. I worked very hard to give her what I thought she deserved. I got everything for her and now she has gone. It does not seem possible. I never knew, you see. I never even suspected. She loved Emily. Do you know that I thought of having an affair with Emily, but I would never betray Charlene. Emily made very direct passes at me, but I kindly refused, and when I was kindly refusing, they were having an affair. I had never even struck another person in my life, but I would have killed them both. I would have killed them both. Should I have killed them both? When I tried to kill myself, it was a way of killing them both. This is true, is it not? I still think of killing them, but I seldom think of killing myself anymore. I would just like to go very far away." Mr. Quimpers circles the initials on the window pane.

"It is very sad. It is very sad that part of what I feel is the humiliation of having other people know that my wife left me for a woman. Every face into which I look is a regurgitation of my shame. I do not want to go out. I do not want to see anyone. Even her mother and father have tried to comfort me. I resent their shame for their daughter and I resent their stupid attempts to tell me they are on my side. What the hell is my side? I have the same side I have always had. Why did she leave me? Why did she leave me for Emily? What is it that Emily provides that I cannot match? I feel all the hate and humiliation every time I have to talk to you. I resent you knowing this thing about me that eats into me. When will you let me out of this so I can hide my shame? I hate the groups where I have to tell this rotten thing to everyone. Here, here is my shame, my stinking garbage pit of shame. Come and look at it. Everyone should know about it. It should be printed in the *Wall Street Journal*. When will you let me go and hide from this horror?"

THE BOMBING OF DRESDEN

There is a smell of magnolias hanging in the air. I am seriously considering buying a large plantation and attacking Fort Sumter. Mr. Tenner sits like a large friendly dog in his chair with a great lopsided smile that sucks in vast amounts of magnolia smells. He makes me happy and sad just to look at him. He is so full of kindness and despair. Mr. Tenner has just made the dean's list at the University of Memphis. He has also switched his major to psychology. This is a common move for college students who are in therapy, and hopefully it will pass.

Soon he will find out that the department of psychology is the worst place for human interaction. Apparently this is like preachers; they have time for everyone but their families. If he thinks his father had no love for him, wait till he meets the staff of the psychology department. Should I tell him what is in store? No, it would serve no purpose but my own.

"Do you like Kurt Vonnegut?" asks Mr. Tenner and smiles into the magnolias.

"Yes I do like Vonnegut. I wish he wrote a book every day."

"Did you read *The Children's Crusade* ? It was very sad. Sometimes I think I like being sad. I know you tell me that my feelings of insecurity come from my father's attitude towards me, but don't you think there are genetic factors too? I mean some people are just born to be sad no matter what happens to them. Isn't this true?"

"I know you have read that it is true, Mr. Tenner, and I believe there are genetic predispositions, but do you really believe that is what has caused your problems?" Gosh, I just love this business.

"No, but I thought it was worth a try. I would like to blame it on something other than my father. I would like to find some DNA with a frown on it. Do you think if you looked very close you would see a tiny frown in the helix?" Mr. Tenner looks out the window at the large neon helix floating in the spring air where the magnolia smell used to hang.

I have tried to get Mr. Tenner's father to come in for some sessions. It was not a victory. "Who the hell did you say you were? Right, you're the guy flim-flaming my son out of his money. Why don't you get a decent job? Better still why don't you get your sanctimonious ass over here and mow my damn yard?" At this point, Mr. Tenner's father hung up. I am so good at this business, but I despise yardwork.

"Do you think that you can blame your father now, Mr. Tenner? We are talking about understanding what happened, not blaming someone. What you do now is up to you. You are no longer a four year old child at the mercy of others." This of course is not true. We are all at the mercy of all that has gone before, but it is what needs to be said.

"I must work it out. That is what we are doing, but sometimes it seems they are dragon's teeth. Every idea I try to rearrange becomes another enemy. I think of what it would be like to have a father that was interested in what I did. I told him I made the dean's list and he said, "Shit happens." I know you have told me that I must try to understand the sadness and despair that motivates him, but it is hard to do sometimes. I know you have told me that I must please myself, that I must work for my own approval, not the approval of others, but it is hard to do. I try to think of things that would finallly make him recognize me. Usually I think of good things, but sometimes I just think of something that would startle him awake to my existence. Sometimes I think I should go to the tower at the university and shoot about twenty people, but I don't own a gun and I don't like them. Do you think the pilots and crews of the bombers understood the horror that they inflicted on the people of Dresden? How could humans do such things to their fellow beings? I don't understand why there is so much horror. I don't understand. If I get a doctorate, do you think it will mean anything to him?"

The Weeds of God

YOU CAN COUNT ON ME

Mr. Meminon has no shoes today. I do not mention this fact and Mr. Meminon does not mention this fact. We are in fact not mentioning it together.

"I love the process of drinking. For some space in my time it begins to make some sense. I like talking with those who see the world through the same window. There seem to be many windows through which the world may be seen and I do not believe mine to be the best, but I cannot talk with any certainty of purpose with those who look through windows I have never seen. It seems I can laugh more at the marvelous madness of it all when there is someone else to share the jokes. I guess some of my best times have been spent in bars with people I admire and respect. There are not too many of these, but the few are magnificent. It is a great feeling of warmth and companionship, a companionship of the similarly damned. I know that it will end as all life ends, in disaster, but I enjoy the moments. Most of the times I have contemplated suicide are when I have been drinking, but I have most thought of living when I have been drinking too. I think it gives courage for one and an excuse for the other, but I am not sure which is which." Two Cathars enter and discuss the Holy Grail and its hiding place. They are still trying to keep it out of Hitler's grasp. How sad.

"I love the song, 'We'll Meet Again.' It always seems to make me happy. I don't even know who I will meet again, but it always makes me happy. It seems so incredibly gentle and sad. Maybe it represents everything any of us lost and how much we would like to return to some real, or imagined time, of magic. "I'll be home for Christmas, you can count on me." That's beautiful too. It whispers of a return to the warmth of those you love. It whispers of the long journey all of us must make. This is a beautiful and horrifying time of year. Christmas is so sad, so joyous. It comes in layers of time each year, layers of Christmases past. I remember all the beautiful times and all the sad times. Sadness falls across me in a quilt of shadows." Mr. Meminon stares out his window at the three wise men who have been hit by a waste disposal truck. There is a hint of frankincense and myrrh in the air.

VALENTINES REMEMBERED

Mr. Guilford has been indicted by the grand jury. The moon no longer shines in the dark night sky and the Mississippi has turned to blood.

Mr. Guilford sits by the window looking out upon a corrupt world that has decided to persecute him. "This whole damn thing is crazy. I haven't done anything that everybody else doesn't do, for God's sake. I can't reach any of my so called friends this morning. Amazing, they were madly in love with me, and now I can't even get through to their offices. I know. I know the voice of a secretary when she's been told not to take a call from someone. It's a very, very lonely feeling. I don't like it. Strange, I remembered all the people that I have done the same thing to. Makes you stop and think. I always thought of them as losers. Now I'm one too. I damn well don't think so. I will find a way out of this shit and be on top again. I won't forget the bastards that turned away. I'll never forget them as long as I live." Mr. Guilford continues on towards Golgotha with his cross. I add a fifty pound weight as he passes and tell my secretary not to take his calls.

"You guys are really sticking it to me. I'm paying over a $1,000 a day for this crap. My lawyer is sticking it to me too. You guys are the cheats. You're making money off my misery. That's cheating. That's cheap, lousy cheating. God, how do you guys stand yourselves. No, I know you have tried to get me discharged and Dr. Mondriatus keeps me in here against your advice. So what? Did you resign? No, you didn't resign, you just keep seeing me and taking the money. Correct? I know it's correct. So you are just as much of a cheat. There seems to be some short perspective all the way around in my opinion." Mr. Guilford stares out the window at the gallows that has been erected on our grassy knoll.

"I have been having the strangest thoughts lately. I thought about a Valentine's party in my third grade class. Mrs. Angelus was my teacher. She was very nice looking. Everybody had to give at least one valentine to someone in the class. Everybody else had Hallmark cards, but we didn't have any money and I was afraid to ask my mother to get a card. I made the card myself. It took three days. I made it out of cardboard from my father's shirts, you know, those pieces of cardboard that came in shirts when they came back from the cleaners. That's what I made it out of. It took me three days and I did all the coloring. It looked good. I mean, I thought it looked good. Mrs. Angelus had all the cards turned in and then she handed them out in front of the class. She handed mine to the girl I had given it to. I don't remember her name, the girl I gave it to. I don't remember her name. She said she didn't want it. She said it was ugly and she didn't want it. I don't remember the girls name, but I hated Mrs. Angelus for letting it happen. I've been thinking about that all morning. I wonder why? I wonder what her name was, the girl who didn't want my Valentine. I can't seem to remember her name." Mr. Guilford has a piece of cardboard in his hands, a piece of cardboard from shirts returned from the laundry. He runs his hands gently over the smooth surface and all the potential beauty that it holds.

INCONTINENCE AND THE VICAR OF CHRIST

Dr. Obviat is quite intoxicated. He is quite lovable too. He makes Will Rogers look like Mark Twain at his worst, and he frequently doubles for Huckleberry Finn. I have painted too many fences for this man. He's not heavy, he's my brother. He is getting a might heavy, however.

Dr. Obviat was arrested for driving under the influence yesterday. He was in my car. He told me he had to go the church to kill the Vicar of Christ. It sounded like a reasonable idea at the time. My car was impounded, but the Vicar escaped.

"Brother, I don't remember exactly what happened," and I believe him. "I was having a very reasonable conversation with the officer until I most casually mentioned the gun. This seemed to be more than he could grasp. I was just trying to be helpful. I thought we were having a friendly talk, so I told him about the gun so he wouldn't be upset when he found it on the floor of the car. That could have been difficult for him. They get very upset when you are carrying a gun. I wonder if he has some massive insecurity problem that he didn't tell me about. At the time he had not discussed a single problem, but I had not really established a sufficient level of rapport. Trust is essential in these situations. This is the very reason I so casually mentioned the pistol. It was not even a large pistol."

Apparently, Dr. Obviat was driving the wrong way down a one-way street with the gull-wings on my DeLorean up and flapping in the breeze. Actually, it is not a bad idea. I never thought of it, but it does look like a great silver bird with wings outstretched. I have caught the wind beneath my wings and reached for the sun. Wax, I hate the amount of wax in this troubled world.

"I am thinking of pleading temporary insanity. I mean that the officer was merely momentarily impaired when he judged me to be intoxicated. I'm a damn psychiatrist for God's sake, and far better at making such a diagnosis. The presumptuous fool. Do I use a radar gun or give parking tickets? You bet your boots I don't."

Dr. Obviat also stuck his finger in the officer's back when the officer was foolish enough to look into the car with his back and Dr. Obviat unattended. Dr. Obviat then stated, "Raise'em high, Elrood, or I'll put so many holes in you I can read my driver's license through your skull." At this point the officer's bowels gave way. Dr. Obviat then stated, "I'm going to write you some script to tighten you up a might, but I can tell you now that you are full of bad humors and need a complete work up when time allows." Dr. Obviat then unzipped his fly and urinated on the side of the squad car. "I hope this makes you feel better. Take this in remembrance of me and the sympathetic union we have reached," said the good doctor. Needless to say, the officer was displeased. Amazingly enough, most of the incident did not appear in the officer's report.

BAD JUDGEMENT FORLORN

Snowmen are melting in my mind. The wind searches pathways across the windowsill and Mr. Arial sits before me, searching for pathways in the windowsill of his mind. I am here too, but forlorn.

"I knew I shouldn't have hit on her. Yeah, I knew that. She was great to look at, maybe a little greater to look at after four martinis. I don't even remember anything until Beth walked in and started to scream." Mr. Arial avoids eye contact and psychomotor agitation is present.

"I love Beth. I can't remember not loving her. I don't even know the other witch's name. I mean it was Darlene or something like Darlene. She wasn't a witch either. I mean, I don't think she was a witch. She sure moved ass when Beth started screaming and hitting her." Mr. Arial is reading something written in his palm. It is hard to read and Mr. Arial takes much time to decipher it. It involves other screams unheard.

"She says she won't take it anymore. You know she moved out. Maybe this time she means it. That's why I'm here. I'm scared of losing her, but I don't have the problem with alcohol she thinks I do. I've got a problem in judgement when it comes to women. That's it. I'll admit whatever you want me to, but that's the real problem and I know it. Bad judgement." Mr. Arial writes "bad judgement" in the snow on the windowsill. The wind comes to look at what Mr. Arial has written and, unimpressed, erases his *mia culpa* for the hope of better things to come.

"You were in your wife's bedroom with Darlene or something, and then your wife and children came home?"

"Yeah, that's it. They came home." Mr. Arial launches into two choruses of "Take Me Home Again Kathleen" and then vomits in the ashtray. I resent that. I would resent it more if I were to deny this. I resent Mr. Arial's denial and I resent the fact that I know I have done the same thing. I am a very resentful man. I most resent that you cannot pass through life without doing harm. Damn.

"You are talking about how bad my judgement was. That's just what I said. Bad judgement."

NEVER QUESTION THE MEATLOAF

"It was some crazy shit," said by Mr. Vediovis with the large scars on his face. I like Mr. Vediovis. I always look him in the face and maintain unblinking eye contact because it is very important to Mr. Vediovis.

The scars on his face are very large, and the one running diagonally across his mouth has created a permanent smile to ward off bad times. People sometimes stare at Mr. Vediovis and this makes him sad. Sometimes people go out of their way to make sure they do not make eye contact with Mr. Vediovis and this makes him sad, too.

I think Mr. Vediovis was born to be happy. Life thought otherwise and has never missed an opportunity to prove the point.

Mr. Vediovis has two children who have definite genetic connections to reptiles. When I see them they are always sitting in chairs next to the window where the sun can warm their blood. I would rather go through Marine Corps bootcamp than spend ten minutes in their company.

"Do you think I am inconsiderate? Why do all these things happen to me? I feel like I am trying to do well. Do you know?" No, Mr. Vediovis, I do not know. Mr. Vediovis always expected to laugh a lot and have good times with a normal family life. He does not understand why so many bad things happen to him, but continues on as if it was only a burp in a restaurant with fine china settings. He has found that alcohol brings back better times. He has also found that alcohol brings back even worse times.

Two years ago, Mr. Vediovis was an insurance salesman who was doing remarkably well. He had money and prestige and a nice home and a nice car and a wife and two children. He laughed a lot and did not seem to notice that his family was on the dysfunctional side of the street. His wife was receiving treatment for depression and both children terrorized their neighborhood, and their classmates and teachers at school. Teachers and students had gotten a fund together to send the Vediovis children to a private school, preferably one with bars on the windows.

Then one night Mr. Vediovis came home and sat down to eat his dinner. The children had already eaten and were upstairs practicing complete revolutions of their heads and spitting green pea soup on the walls. Mr. Vediovis took a bite of his meatloaf and then asked if he could have some pepper for the meatloaf. He did not say the meatloaf was bad or that it usually came in slices rather than heaps. He did not say that he would rather have something else or that he thought that having meatloaf four times a week was somewhat excessive. Mrs. Vediovis said she would be right back to spice up the meatloaf and then went upstairs.

Just as Mr. Vediovis was taking a sip of his ice-tea, Mrs Vediovis appeared at the door with a twenty-two caliber automatic pistol. She then stated, "This should spice it up a bit." She fired eight shots at Mr. Vediovis' head, hitting him with four.

When Mr. Vediovis awoke, there were a number of police officers who wanted to question him. Mrs. Vediovis had been taken to the psychiatric hospital after a short stay in jail. Apparently even the jail was not prepared for questions concerning her meatloaf.

Mr. Vediovis refused to file charges and tried to claim that he had shot himself. Mr. Vediovis has claimed all of the bad times. There was a time when he could turn them inside out and make it better, but those times have begun to fade.

People seemed to blame Mr. Vediovis for the incident. How could he be a good person if his wife wanted to kill him so much? If things are this bad, is he not to blame? Can you get shot standing next to him and can all this bad luck not rub off on someone who deals with him? Mr. Vediovis was indicted by the accidents of time, and his willingness to accept them. I never question anyone about meatloaf unless I am wearing a bulletproof vest and packing iron.

Now Mr. Vediovis never questions the bourbon and water that waiters bring him, even if it tastes like scotch. Mr. Vediovis waits for the next disaster and tries to find the laughter and courage he once held. He just keeps trying, and he accepts his children as they are, and goes to see his wife on the psychiatric ward every single visiting day, but he never questions the meatloaf.

MR. HENLEY'S DREAMS

"My mother is spanking me and a large bird is flying around her head. I am not scared. There is a box of large, very large, Tootsie-Rolls that is also flying around the room. I like Tootsie-Rolls. The room is filled with water, but it is the color of beer. Gogi Grant is singing "The Wayward Wind" and all sorts of things are floating in the yellow water: money, large bills, garter-belts, large flashlights, and little ships." Mr. Henley is discussing his dream of last night. He has seen movies and believes he should be sharing this with me. Freud and Jung have coughed and left the room. Not together.

Freud and Jung were wonderful shamans to cast other's dreams on the floor of the hut and read there in the mystery of their patient's lives. The same themes and archetypes fill every culture and every mythology. For thousands of years the dreams have been the same, but what of Neanderthal. Were their dreams the same?

Freud and Jung's interpretations fell out of favor even before they could be faced with Mr. Henley. The profession now believes most of these marvelously convoluted mirrors of reality are only random firings of neurons. Yes, dreams are just screen savers for the mind. All the beautiful allegories and juxtapositions of possibility are only biochemical standby modes. Dreams can address problem solving, or a need to get up and urinate, or a desire to sleep just a little longer, but they are just small accidents with meaningless written in big letters on the screen. Jung laughs and makes the mantra for warding off small stupidities while dreaming that Freud's mouth is stuffed with many small pebbles. He is, after all, a member of the royal family.

"There is a clown with a large bullhorn sticking out of his groin. He starts to sing. I do not know what he is singing. His mouth is very, very large. There is a wind in my shorts." Shut up, Mr. Henley or I will kill you myself.

I believe my dreams are more than random firings of neurons. Sometimes they are more real and meaningful than the other side of sleep. And when I dream and know I am dreaming, who is it that knows the dream from the dreamer? Will these configurations of energy and matter not be held in some form forever changing? Nothing ceases, it only changes.

Shiva has danced in me, Thor's hammer has forged parts of my soul, Athena has held me safe, Dagda has winked in my night, and I have seen Ragnarok and Crumcrulak in dreams that fold in upon me as the pages of a book upon its spine. All of this is me and what will be me.

FENRER NEVER STOPS HERE

It is very cold. The place seems heavy with the sadness of winter. I wish to give the world back the laughter of summer. I wish many things. There are so many things I would like to do that would be good for everyone. I make lists of them. Some of them I actually accomplish. Why are there so many that I never complete? Almost every patient wishes the same things, at least they seem to wish such things. They seem to wish more than those who do not sit across the desk from me. Is this a great insight? Is this what forces the contortions in their minds, this hope to make a difference, this hope to make it better for all the sad shadows that play around us? It is very cold and my wishes fall helpless at winter's feet.

Today is my chart day. I write my weekly progress notes on this sacred day. I hate having to write in these damn charts. You must attempt to explain what you are doing. What am I doing? Who do we help? At least it gives them some small respite from the cold. Soon the same words come over and over again. I have written this sentence a thousand times, and I have seen the same patient a thousand times. Will these magic words give them any help? No. It serves only to fulfill the demands of those who pretend to evaluate and sanction our services. It is such a strange business, so full of sadness, so full of charlatans and the sick leading the sicker. None of us could have even been contenders and it is very cold. I can see the cold from my window, my great aquarium window that holds out the world in which they live.

Ragnarok will be unknown here. Fenrer will not notice us. All will pass us by for we are meaningless in the conflict. One way or another we have removed ourselves from the fray. I long to fight on the side of righteousness. I wish to stand with others feeling the bond of belief that runs through us. I wish to know we fight for all those too weak to stand, for all those so easily trampled under the feet of indifference. I wish a life full of meaning, but it is very cold and the charts must be filled.

I LOVE HER TOO, MR. HILLARD

It is cold in the land of Lorn and widows weep over the bones of the slain. The cold fills me and I dream of a quilt of sunshine laying across my fields. Mr. Hillard is droning on about his wife's infidelities and the sorrows these have wrought. Mrs. Hillard should be disowned, but Mr. Hillard loves the sadness that she brings for it is so in keeping with all he believes.

"I really love her. That's the problem. I love her more than she loves me. She says she loves me and then she whores around."

Indeed that is the problem, we all love her more than she can love. But then maybe this is why we love her so, for she washes us with her unbounded sadness.

IMPERIUM

What is this all about? Sometimes, in the corner of my eye, I think I have located the key that winds the toy, but it simply falls away. It simply falls away and nothing lures it back. Was it there? Sadness seems to be what this world is about. Broken things running riot in my landscape. Yes, there are moments of great joy and moments of triumph, but they cannot be held and slip beneath the waves that hide a sea of discarded time. Why is it not possible to hold and savor these moments, to rest within them and slide them up and down across the tongue? Why do they pass so quickly into the dark and who gets them when they are gone? Is there a warehouse in time that holds these moments waiting for the man from the lost and found? Why must this go on?

"What would take its place?" Caesar has his stripped toga and red shoes. Caesar is unafraid for he holds the imperium and I only hold a degree in psychology. Psychology is divided into three parts: before Freud, during Freud and Freud behind the times.

Why do we give such pain? We cannot seem to get it right.

RAMESES REVISITED

Good morning Mr. Epstein, the only emotionally disturbed Jew in Memphis, and how are you today? We must discuss the Sabbath and why you have ruined Friday nights. Lets drink one to Ramases II and his total insouciance concerning the Jewish problem. Let us part the Red Sea and piss in a silver bowl.

"Good morning doctor. It's another lovely day in our neighborhood," says Mr. Epstein. I feel there is a level of levity in Mr. Epstein this morning. Mr. Epstein has been having a drinking problem. He has been having a fornication problem. He has been having a wife problem.

Mr. Epstein's wife comes from a very wealthy family. They bought Mr. Epstein's dreams when he married Rebecca. They keep his dreams in an earthen jug in their smallest bathroom and laugh a lot when they see them. They pay for his very large office in a very expensive building in a very expensive area of the city. Mr. Epstein is a lawyer and the family needed a good Jewish lawyer.

Mr. Epstein's wife caught him with another woman. Even worse, the woman was a gentile. Does no one have any sense of decency? Now he has a gentile therapist. Is there no end to what the man must suffer?

Mr. Epstein's wife indicated that he was about to become the only poor Jew on their block unless he did exactly what she said. Mr. Epstein took this seriously and pleaded that he was intoxicated during the entire episode. Three glasses of Manashevitz, and every *shiksa* looks appealing. Besides, you know what they are like. As punishment, Mrs. Epstein sentenced him to our unit because she knows a good thing when she sees it.

If you look at our intakes, you will not find a Jewish name for the past twenty years except Mr. Epstein. We have listed him as Manshevitz Shiksa Epstein Syndrome.

Mr. Epstein will be gone soon. He will only stay about five days. This is the appropriate sentence for Manashevitz Shiksa Epstein Syndrome. Mr. Epstein will see five days in hell every time he looks at another inviting lady. Mr. Epstein will also learn to be more circumspect in such dealings. This was Mr. Epstein's first fall from grace. There were three exacerbating variables in the incident: the woman was a *shiksa*, he was blatantly clumsy in his assignation producing questions concerning his syllogistic reasoning abilities and delivering a direct insult to the whole family, and he could not produce even the semblance of an interesting excuse when caught. Yahweh hates the unimaginative sinner for he has no saving grace.

Mrs. Epstein has refused to see Mr. Epstein while he is on the unit. She has allowed him to write a number of fawning letters, however. These are graded for content, imagination, style and spelling and returned to Mr. Epstein. Mr. Epstein is paying me $100 a letter to write these for him. Finally he is developing a sense of proportion. He is also beginning to take an interest in Nurse Brunhilde and writing witty things on the bathroom wall. All of this bodes well for the future.

YELLOW SAILS

Mr. Edwards is talking. The sun is curling around my fingers on the desk. It is warm. Mr. Edwards is talking. The sun is spinning a cocoon around my mind. Mr. Edwards is talking. Mr. Edwards is disturbing the cocoon. Is something meaningful about to be said? Do not do it, Mr. Edwards. Not now. I am like a fighter resting a round before I go all out in the tenth. I am accepting the despoiling of my mind with trivialities. Wait, my mind is a sea of trivialities. No, it is a matter of beloved trivialities as opposed to the trivialities of others. Yes, I am on the right track here. Mr. Edwards is talking.

"I like being in here sometimes. It gives me time to think about things, different things from what I normally think about. My business is going well. I am really good at my business. I've got two crews working now on three different jobs. Even from in here I can get all of it done. It's really not that hard, but most people don't know how easy it is. On small jobs I don't even estimate really, I just kind of guess. I think this is what most contractors do. It is really easy to make money when you know what you are doing . I'm making a lot more money than most people that graduated from college. My family is well taken care of. I can tell you that."

There is an inland sea on which I float. The sail is yellow, a very violent yellow that screams at the sun. Fish jump through holes in the surface of the sea and send suggestions of their accomplishments wandering away. I do not wish to catch them, only to believe in their presence and their cities beneath the sea.

I feel depressed. Is this situational? Is anything not situational and what is my situation? What is the meaning of all this crap? Nothing good seems to be sustainable. The world is full of so much pain and misery. It is a damn horror. Each of us by the very nature of our flesh must pass through one foolish humiliation after another until death parts us from all the threats that abound. Sometimes I am sick to death of it. After a night of libation and gaiety, the next day brings a gray world of no hope. I know, it is a deficiency of B-1, Vitamin C, and Vitamin A. This is even more terrifying. Is it all just a matter of the levels of serotonin, endorphins, and myriad micro-possibilities within my blood stream that cause happiness, hope and despair? Jesus Christ. And what of the enjoyment of sadness itself?

"You make it too complex. What you are asking is meaningless. You know it is meaningless because you know there is no answer for you to the questions you ask. The functioning of the organism is the organism. That is it. Stop and the organism stops. Act happy and you will increase the chances of happiness. Act sad and you will increase the chances of sadness. As you view the event, you change the event. If you view it as happy, you will change the event itself because, for you, the event exists only in your mind." Why Gaius Julius Caesar and not Jung? Why have I found Caesar? Because my view changed the event? What event? Are there not an infinite number of events within any split second of what I believe to be time?

"There is much to be said for the immediate possibility of danger or the ever present need to act in order to survive. Your thoughts are the luxuries of a civilization grown fat with time on its hands. It is not that attempting to unravel the mysteries that surround us is useless or self-defeating, on the contrary, but it is to say that unraveling imaginary threads just for the enjoyment of unraveling them serves no purpose other than filling up useless time. Hold to what is meaningful, meaningful in that it reshapes thought, or changes behavior, or rearranges the building blocks of matter and energy to create that which will enrich your life or the life of others. All else is meaningless drivel."

Do you remember Brutus, you ass? What sense does any of that make? What acts of kindness you had given to him. How he betrayed you and yet you bandy words about rearranging the building blocks of energy. Would you not rather rearrange the building blocks of Brutus' skull?

"What you ask has nothing to do with our discussion, it has only to do with your irritation with your situational depression. As for Brutus, I have had time to understand and he struck at what he saw which I can now also see. I would, however, happily in the moment rearrange numerous skulls, and in resurrecting that past, I would have struck before their minds could will their actions, but that was long ago and dearly forgotten. And that is mine alone and done, whereas yours is yet to be. Will you use your dagger to slay yourself and be your own Brutus?"

THE ABDUCTION OF KINDNESS

Mr. Nemoria does not seem to know I am present. He talks candidly, avoids eye contact, and addresses the Ficus Benjamina in the corner. The Ficus appears interested, but is known for a general, and well-founded, bias towards the species.

Mr. Nemoria is an episodic alcoholic who comes voluntarily to our sacred shrine once or twice a year. He does not get in trouble with the law and he lives in an old picture book of heroes he once read in the attic with his grandmother holding his hand and smiling gently into his mind.

"I know I cannot love like others love. I like taking care of people, but I am never really close to them, and I never let them know my real fears and desires." The Ficus looks interested still, and more accepting of possible truths.

"I remember living with my grandparents when I was a child. At the time, I thought they were my parents. My father had died, and my mother had left me with my grandparents while she worked far away in a city beneath the sea.

"We lived on a large farm with large people and large animals. It was a nice place to be, a very nice place to be. My grandparents were strong and powerful and kind. I remember feeling very safe and very loved. I have never felt that way since, since I was taken away.

"We worked on the farm six days a week. We worked together in the fields picking cotton, corn and soybeans. We worked together in the planting too. I was so small, but I knew I was part of a family, a family that held each other close and safe.

"During the week there were no other children to play with, for no one lived within three miles of us. On Sundays, all the clan would gather, uncles and aunts, nieces and nephews, and eat huge meals cooked by all the ladies of the clan. There were wonderful games to play and a huge farm to wander within.

"I remember being so happy and content. I was part of something, something that went on and on endlessly, something that would never end. Each member of the clan had appointed tasks and a part to play in the maintenance of order, stability and contentment.

"There was an immense feeling of pride in being part of the clan. I was never lectured on honor or integrity or what was expected. When I acted against an ethical principle, I was told what was wrong and how to correct the behavior. It was totally expected that I would follow the directives. Most of all, there were continuing examples of honesty and ethical behavior all around me. I was surrounded by those who would be good and expected to act in accordance with these concepts. I was a part of a group in which I could take pride and within which I felt a contributing member. I was not alone. I was not alone. I was valued. I was safe within the strength of the clan.

"Then one day, they came for me. My mother and my stepfather came for me. They were lovely people, young and lovely people. They had come before, three or four times a year, they had come before. They brought candy and games from the big city in which they lived so far away beneath the sea. They dressed differently from us and they spoke differently from us because they came from beneath the sea.

"My grandparents tried to explain that I was going someplace else to live. I was six years old and I knew no other place except in books, about people who lived beneath the sea. My grandparents looked very sad, but they spoke directly without hesitation or emotion and I knew that it must be. I thought it must be something I must do, as if a chore assigned to help the clan.

"I sat in the back seat of a large, new car and looked out the back window at my grandparents standing in the yard. Somehow they did not look as big as I had always seen them before, as if they were pulled by time into some other place unknown. I watched them standing in the yard waving until I could no longer make them out in the distance down the long straight road. I did not cry and I did not speak of my great and utter sadness, for members of the clan do not show such things to strangers.

"There is no blame in such things, as there is no blame in the tornado that rips up the roots of a tree. All too frequently there is no right in a situation, only shades of sadness and despair, some of which hopefully will lead to better times.

"On that day, the clan gave me up to strangers from beneath the sea. I will never love again as I loved before. I will never trust again as I trusted before. I will never feel as safe or content again, but I will hold the honor of the clan and not cry in front of strangers . . . and I will keep the faith."

The Ficus is crying. The Ficus is crying for he no longer stands amongst the clan where the true rain falls from the sky and the earth is what it will always be and not some potting soil from the store beneath the sea.

BATTLES LEFT UNANSWERED

I have heard all these damn stories before. I need new material, new twists and turns of intricate sadness that will befuddle the mind.

Hang yourself, brave Freud, we fought and you were not there. There is a vast unseen battlefield all around us stretching as far as the eye can see. Bodies are heaped one upon the other in perfect symmetry and squalor. This is the most perfect of all worlds. Sadness in a million forms blooms across a meadow reaching for the stars. Who framed this perfect symmetry? Not I. I would have been kinder by far.

"It's not my fault. Jesus, I hit her because she hit me. Not with her fist, but with a million words that smashed my mind. I smashed the table first, then I smashed the plates. She always picks the kitchen to start this shit. She wants to make sure that I'll always remember when I eat. She wants everything to be bad, even frankfurters. I don't even remember what the argument started with. I know, I had been drinking, but I know she was wrong. She kept coming at me and beating me down, over and over like the drip of a giant faucet on your soul. I tried to get away from her, but she followed like the hound from hell. I'm scared. I felt like killing her. It was so hard to stop. I just hit her once, but I know I could have hit her a thousand times until there was only blood and bone. Now I'm sorry, so damn sorry, but I know she wanted to hurt me as bad as I wanted to hurt her. I know she wanted to see blood and bone. I know she felt good when she knew I felt horrified by what I had done. I know that. I want to leave her and I want to stay. I feel so sorry for her. I know she has been hurt by life, and I know she fights on, but I hate her when she takes it out on me and I hate myself for all of it." I take Mr. Wainscoat into the kitchen and we fix some frankfurters with lots of ketchup. Mr. Wainscoat is crying and it gets in the ketchup, but I do not mention it.

You must leave her, Mr. Wainscoat. You must leave for sure. Yet, I know you will return to this bed of sorrow for the bonds are great indeed. You have shared disaster after disaster with this one and she is bound within your mind as long as you shall live. It is so intense, so

The Weeds of God 157

marvelously intense. It is hard to find such intensity, and sorrow is so much easier to share than joy. Joy cannot compete with the force of the scream within you or the tornado of emotions you catalyze.

It drips upon the soul from a great height, one after the other never ending always falling never ceasing. Even with eyes closed, the sound is there, always falling never ceasing. There is not that much ketchup left in the world, Mr. Wainscoat. Run, run, Mr. Wainscoat, from that damned kitchen or you will forever dine on frankfurters, guilt and pain.

The Weeds of God

ACCEPT OR ACT

Do not talk with me. Leave me in the peace of my own turmoil.

"You are enjoying your own turmoil. You who can so easily see through the glass houses of others, refuses to look into your own. I do not say that there are not great questions, only that screaming into yourself when you find one does not produce solutions." Caesar holds a copy of *The Weeds of God*. I wonder what page he was reading. Where do I fall from each page and why?

Caesar drinks no wine, not even watered wine does Caesar drink. There are some things more easily seen in the bottom of the cup. Will Caesar not ever see these? Why is it so easy for you, Caesar? No, you only give the facade we all show to the thorns upon the rose. You too wonder. I do not know which I would rather believe.

"Then believe them both, or believe in waves from one to the other as thought allows. Do you think it will make the slightest difference? I once loved Brutus with great clarity, and still love as the waves weep from one crest to the next. It makes no difference. Only what I will makes a difference. Happiness, contentment and completion are the individual creations of a single mind. You create what you feel. None should know better than you."

I knew Brutus made a difference. I knew you wept for him. This indeed I knew. I too have wept for such things. I have even wept at my own betrayals. I weep still. There seems no end to them even with the best of intent. No end.

"You want to be a vegetarian, do you not? No, bear with me for this is the point. I see you agonize over the death of those animals that come prepared so sweetly to your table. You know the horrible deaths that consumed their lives. You eat of their flesh. You think it wrong, but fail each time you try to renounce this abomination. You writhe in the throws of the dilemma. If you were a vegetarian, then you would be a butcher of plants. How do you know they do not feel, too? Why do you contort you own mind in such a fashion? Either accept or act. To stop the butchery, you must act against those who perpetuate it. Destroy the plants that kill animals. Strike against stores that sell meat. Strike against restaurants that squander the flesh of once living beings to satisfy those already fat with the bounty of the earth. But if you do, what will become of all these animals? If we do not kill and eat them, then how will we provide for them? They will fill the earth in their millions, eating all before them. There will be millions of them, or should we sterilize them? Will we set up thousands of sterilization stations for them? Have we the right to sterilize these beings? Each solution creates its own new problem. Do not sit and squander the time you still possess. Either accept or act. Nothing is wrong with either, but constantly shuffling decks of philosophical dreck is wasteful beyond measure and serves no purpose. Accept or act, that is all one needs to know. *Solvitur ambulando.*"

I knew you wept for Brutus. I knew that well.

THE UNCERTAINTY OF UNCERTAINTY

God is the principal of uncertainty. This seems relatively certain. There is a certainty of uncertainty looming in the air. There are speeds greater than the speed of light. The capillary streams of subatomic particles do not act with certainty until they reach the veins of the macrocosm. Here they obediently follow their appointed route to the sea. But are all things written still?

Across time and space particles can change their identity instantaneously when their twin is changed. Entanglement. How do they know? How can they change instantly? What links these twins no matter how separated across vast distances? What force makes this demand and writes these changes in the universal log?

I tell you I am baffled and gladly so. Maybe all things are not written. Maybe we are not the simple sum of genetics and environment. Maybe there is more, but I despair to believe it. Each day parades a million stimuli to which I respond based on my past, and the next day will lead me on to a certain path. Those around me stumble on as I.

I hear their words and I am desperately sad. They have been created and are forced to accept their own creation. Most follow blindly without knowledge of their fate. The most appalling horror is saved for those whose intellect allows vast reflection on their own being. The more they look, the greater their fear and dread.

I can only see the macrocosm. Where is that beautiful flow of uncertainty? I need to hear the sound of the dice being thrown. As I grow older, I love more and more the turn of a card. I know the probabilities, but each game is a new beginning, a new life to live on each card that falls to my hand.

Somehow each card falling seems more of me than all the things I have set a hand to and gained or lost. It falls without realization of the hand that sends it on its way or the hand that will receive it. It falls with the grace of uncertainty. It wishes nothing of me, nor does it presume upon what I wish of it.

They come here to speak of what they have known of time. It has shaped them with great presumption, this river that flows from their past. Some are determined to fight and others are determined to seek salvation wherever the river will take them. They are all, however, part of the river and they can only act within the boundaries of the river's course. I have seen the river and I am part of it.

I would sing the body electric too, but I have learned too much and too little of its nature. There are some things better left unknown and some doors of the mind better left unopened. I say this with the certainty that I feel now, though I know this certainty will be shaped again and again by the river until my energy is conserved in some other form I cannot know.

MRS. LIPPON'S SEXUAL DRAGONS

Mr. Lippon is morose. Yes, not less rose but mo rose. Mr. Lippon is having a near-life experience.

I am having a battle with outsomnia and can barely find my place in his thoughts. This goes on simultaneously with the Chinese drill team working on the roof. I love this damn place.

"I can't seem to get a grip on it. Why? I don't know. I mean, I don't know. My wife won't have sex with me. I mean, sometimes she just lays there, but that's it. She just lays there. I mean, what does it mean? I ask her and she says there is nothing wrong, but I don't think so. I mean, is this normal? Do they all just lay there?" The Chinese drill team punctuates the process with what sounds like one of them falling through the roof. That is indeed a nice touch. Should I go see? No, greater minds than mine are undoubtedly working on the problem. Besides the other noises of hammering have temporarily ceased. He gave his life that others might live. I shall see a medal is granted and a plaque suitably engraved for the occasion.

"Do you think women like sex? I mean, I have known ones that seem a lot more enthusiastic. Do you see what I'm saying? It seems like she is just going through the motions." I hear a Chinese funeral in the distance. There are firecrackers and dragons and still Mrs. Lippon just lays there.

"I go out and drink and it's not so bad. I just get on her for a couple of minutes and that's it. I mean, then I just go to sleep. She just goes to the bathroom. What do they do in the bathroom? She always looks like I took something from her. I just want sex like a natural man. Isn't that a normal thing? Since we had the child, she has had no interest in sex. I know you told me about why it might be like that, but how long do I have to wait? Shouldn't she be getting help? Maybe there's some drug you could give her that would put some zip back in it. I just want it to be nice again. I know she has to take care of the kid, but why does that tire her out so much? I help when

I can. Sometimes I feel she thinks I don't help at all, but I help when I can. I mean, I'm tired when I get home. She should think about that. She never thinks about me. Everything is centered on the child. I mean, I love him, but you have to share these things out. She is just thinking about herself and the child. She doesn't think about what I need anymore. I mean, I have needs too."

Mrs. Lippon is having sex with the Chinese drill team. She is very excited. They are all wearing dragon outfits and do not smell of stale beer and yesterday's dreams. They smell of fire-crackers and consideration because they work on the roof all day and are happy to please a woman when they find one.

One to say mass
One to forego
One for direction
And one to say go
Two to find more
And three to make four
One to tell when
To make all a then
And some to give flavor
To all that has been
But none can explain
Either pleasure or pain

CAESAR'S SOLILOQUY

Give it a rest, Caesar. Go talk to your wife who is above reproach. Why do I never see her by the way? Has she learned to shop at Tiffany's and does she drive a Ferrari? Does she secretly wish to be the mother of the Gracchi?

"If you did not wish to hear from me, you would not summon me. Your time is near. I know this and you know this. You could do so much if you would only allow yourself to follow the path you truly believe. What you rebel against are the very threads that hold the tapestry of time together. Without adversity, sadness, brutality, despair, injustice and all the myriad horrors that befall your lot there would be only a singularity – a blackhole of mediocrity, a flat line of concentrated meaninglessness, a mathematical formula of infinite zeroes. There would be neither questions, nor answers, only a herd of automatons grazing on an endless sea of perfect grass.

All is alive and all is conflict. Whether rock or rock star, we pulse within an infinity of possibilities. Nothing is lost and nothing forgotten. How many paths will you walk down before you rest with your beliefs?

How many philosophical roads you have traveled to find some meaning to it all when you only have to accept. You have sought so desperately for the cessation of worldly desire, but giving these up to empty contemplation of empty contemplation is only an exclamation of meaninglessness. There is no loyalty without the temptation to betray, no courage without the realization of fear, no joy without the possibility of despair, no kindness without the shadow of meanness, no love without hate, and no life without the imminence of death. Loss of libido can be accomplished with medication, but neither medication, nor meditation can accomplish the goals you seek.

You have even thought of accepting the immediacy of your own desires and acting on every whim of evil that passes through your mind. It is not better, however, to reign in hell than to serve in heaven because you cannot serve in hell. The essence of God is servitude, servitude to the concept of perfection within all things great and small. You know this. You have felt it before and held it, only to turn away because there is so much to hold and such a fear of failure." Caesar, my beloved, you have been reading Gorgias again, but missed the eristical parts that you would have so loved. I am tired of self and selflessness. Let us go forth to Gaul and divide it into three parts for the hell of it.

The Weeds of God

THE MONKEY DOES NOT LIE

Mr. Lincoln is not feeling well today. He has finished his detoxification regimen and it has finished him. Mr. Lincoln would like a drink. Just one drink would set him right and one drink more and on into that dark night. Every whiskey river must run dry. That is a sadness. It can never continue at just that right mix of being in control and being out of control. Out of control weighs in and your ship sinks. Nothing lovely continues forever and then there is a price to pay. You have used up a lot of good times and the gods demand an accounting. An equal or greater share of bad times must be payed. The bad times get so bad, and you know you can find some good times back in the river and you fall again into those gentle waves of laughter missed.

I know Mr. Lincoln, I know. Why should you have to work so hard at having good times, when they are just a liquor store away? Why spend all the hours it takes to gain joy from the grudging hands of time when it can be found so easily? Besides, you will fail anyway, so why waste the time?

I know Mr. Lincoln, I know. You have tried before and hoped before. You have watched those who hoped with you and counted on you. Each time there is more reason to go back to the river where nothing is asked except capitulation. The faces of those you have betrayed will fade. All despair will be blunted. Nothing will be quite as bad as you thought. Many funny things will be said. There will be laughter and you can sleep in your own little bed again. But it cannot be sustained and love and laughter will fade. Each time you fall back into the river there is more reason to go back to the river where such things are momentarily washed away.

"I'm going to do it this time. You won't see me in here again. I'm never going through this again. Never again." Mr. Lincoln opens his second pack of the day and sucks the very heart from a Marlboro Light. The monkey on Mr. Lincoln's back smiles and lights up too. The monkey nods his head, blows some smoke towards the ceiling and smiles again. The monkey and I are old friends. He has his job and I have mine. I like the monkey because sometimes he means well and he does not lie. Sometimes I lie and sometimes Mr. Lincoln lies, but the monkey does not lie.

"I know it will be different this time. You are really helping a lot. I know that I can't have that first drink because that's the first step to being drunk. I know that now. It's taken me a long time, but I really know that now." Mr. Lincoln seems to shimmer as if seen across a desert's heat, as if he was being focused in a great pair of unseen binoculars. The monkey looks very sad.

"This time I have a plan. Like you said, I have got to think ahead and not put myself in positions that will lead me back to it. It slips up on you and then it's got you again. That's what I've got to watch. This time I'm going to do it. I'm going to make it this time and you won't see me again." The monkey looks very sad and the monkey does not lie.

"You have really helped me. I just can't fall back." Mr. Lincoln falls back into the chair and the monkey disappears.

I am tired, very tired. I walked fifteen hours on the Bataan Death March accompanied by W.C. Fields and Mae West. They complained frequently and never shared their water. I no longer love the Japanese army and their code of Bushido sucks. We need to play some hockey with these guys. Put them on skates and they are lost. A few good checks into the wall and we can score thirty goals on the runts. Gordie Howe could take the whole team on by himself. Where are you, Gordie?

"I'm feeling much better today, much better. I don't even think about having a drink and that's the truth." I am thinking about having a drink, Mr. Edsut. I am thinking about it seriously and I would never lie about this to you. We missed you. You were not on the march and even W.C. made a comment or two about your lack of involvement. Mae was strangely silent. It makes one wonder.

"I'm beginning to get my head straight. I guess I'm beginning to know what is important, or I'm beginning to see what is really important." So now you are coming around. A little damn late. The march is over and you never showed up. We missed you. Why are you wearing a rubber band stretched across your eyes? And why have you put on thick glasses and a set of buck teeth? And why are you wearing leggings and eating only at sushi bars, you vermiverous swine?

"My son doesn't really understand what is going on. He's too young. That's good because it really hasn't had an effect on him." We carried your son with us, Mr. Edsut. Even W. C. carried him for a while although he complained vehemently that the child had stolen his booze and two of his best one-liners. He was there and you were not. He will remember, Mr. Edsut. There will always be small swirls of memory that touch him when he least expects it. He will remember that you were not there and he will wonder. He will wonder if he was not good enough to deserve your love and loyalty. It will color all he does. He will forget the Japanese. He will forget the thirst, but he will remember that you were not there for him and there will be a bright flash of sadness and shame.

It is alright for he in his turn will betray as we all do, and he will understand better and forgive more easily, but he will remember your absence. Each of us must inevitably join the association of betrayers, the largest brotherhood on the planet. There are different levels of betrayal, however, and there are some like shreds of glass in a clenched fist.

"You see, I never meant to hurt anyone. I know I mostly hurt myself. I guess that's obvious, but I'm just learning it." The Japanese guards turn away in shame and begin reading their books on the MacArthur Plan. Even they participated, but you gave only your absence. Few things fill up the libraries of sadness like the Books of Absence.

The Weeds of God

I THE PLANET

I have the flu. I am full of foreign bodies. An army of phagocytes does battle in the darkness. Who are these people?

Vast armies fight by night within the roads and crossroads of life within me. Do they have individual heroes who rally faltering troops to stem the tide of battle? Does Epaminondas lead with wit and honor against those who were never beaten before. Will some unknown Sulla win the crown of crass today?

Within my veins more battles are fought than ever the outside world will see. I seldom give them thought, yet they hold the dogs of war at bay, and sacrifice themselves in battle after battle unto death. They die that others may live; that I may continue. Do they know for what or whom they fight? Is there honor here and loyalty, or only the minute mechanics of life? I know they too have names and aspirations of joy, and I thank them for such dedication. They hold the planet, the homeland, against the never ending storm of invaders. They stand and my foundations stay. What the gods abandon, they defend and save the some of things today.

Each of these tiny entities has a life all its own. How am I the sum of all these billions of lifes? I am affected by each of these and they by me, but are we one and the same? I know of them, but do they know of me? Am I just a vast universe in which they wander? They have their appointed rounds and I mine. Sometimes they do not function well and sometimes I do not function well.

What is time like for them, I wonder. Do they know they are composed of atoms and myriad sub-atomic particles driven by the mystical forces of existence?

All of these billions upon billions of entities that are me, do they understand string theory any better than I? Am I simply a single cell within God? Does God have the flu, too?

THE CLAN OF THE CAVE BEAR

My eyes hurt. All my eyes hurt. Many eyes are hurting. Hurt hurls itself inside my mind through the portals of my eyes. Little porcupines of pain are dancing in my eyes. Drink is a curse. I know this now, but in two days I will forget and try to paint a better picture of the world in an alcohol based medium.

Mr. Danzer paints with morphine and dabs of madness unrequited. I like Mr. Danzer because he is great fun to listen to and every session is an opportunity for him to use the material that has grown stale for close acquaintances. I am getting years of material in these sessions. We have uncovered material down to the Mesozoic. Alexander presses on towards India and the man who would be treated as a king.

"My wife's family has just reached the Stone Age. When I am forced to go to their hovel, you can see the joy of knowing they cannot only keep a fire going indefinitely, but have tools that can be used more than once. The last time I was there, the whole family was painting pictures of bison on the ceiling. I could hear Margaret Mitchell behind the walls. If they find her, they will sacrifice her to one of their lesser gods and eat her. I never use a lighter in their presence because of the prime directive." Mr. Danzer fidgets constantly because his body, each cell alone and in concert, searches for the magic drug we have denied him. Where has the beautiful lady gone? I know what pictures you would paint on the wall, Mr. Danzer.

"They think painting should only be done to lure the souls of the beasts on which they prey. They ask when I will go to work in the quarry or become a great hunter and stop this foolishness. Irene must have been adopted. The tribe probably found her wandering on the steppes and captured her. I wonder sometimes why she does not notice that she is the only member of the tribe without a large ridge over her eyes. The fact that none of the others walks upright should have given her a clue. I have never asked her because I am a coward and I am so afraid of losing her. She is all I have. I love her and I am amazed by it, amazed and very happy. You know that I am fifteen years older than Irene. She does not seem to notice, just like she missed the excessive amount of facial hair her brother Quibe sports and his inability to count without using small pebbles."

Mr. Danzer was arrested for purchasing morphine from the wrong person. He is forty-five years old and teaches at the art academy. His paintings are full of color and laughter. He tried to give me one, but I had to return it because Nurse Nightingale saw him and she is part of the Cave Bear Clan. Mr. Danzer drives a completely restored, night-black 1957 Ford Thunderbird and his wife, Irene, is tall and beautiful and loves him very much. That was good enough for me. Mr. Danzer's lawyer drives a Cadillac and wants to be counsel for the Cave Bear Clan. " Look, you and I know the score. Keep him for twenty days and he walks. Everybody is happy. You get paid and my client doesn't do any time. We all got this straight?" Yes, I believe I have it, but my eyes hurt like hell. It is from seeing such things and knowing you should be smoking a small cigar and we should not be in this movie. I want another movie. Let us shop for a good movie to be in that has an excessively happy ending, maybe many endings, all excessively happy. Maybe we should give morphine to all of the members of the Cave Bear Clan and see what happens. Think of the new paintings they could do on the wall and on the Cadillac.

NO LIGHT AT THE END OF THE TUNNEL

Mrs. Ramases has read a new article in *Psychology Today*. She should not have read it. We should not leave such possibilities lying around the unit for unsuspecting patients to fall upon.

The article explains that near-death experiences can be explained by brain functions that are common to our species. Basically the article indicates that any of us experiencing oxygen loss and shock have a mechanism that can produce the sensations associated with near-death experiences — a sense of calm, a feeling of leaving our bodies to float as an energy mass, a visual experience of seeing a bright light suggesting a destination of considerable merit, and a general feeling of euphoria with the suggestion of better things to come. Jesus, what an ass. Why would anyone want to take this possibility of immortality and rapture from our grasp? Is this man a Jesuit? Must God sort them out?

Mrs. Ramases is depressed. I am depressed. Mrs. Ramases lost her right arm and her only daughter in a car accident some two years ago. She was pinned in the wreck and watched her daughter bleed to death while the driver of the other car wandered drunkenly around the wreckage with no apparent injuries. She had a near-death experience on the operating table. It is one of the few bits of experience that have kept her relatively intact.

Mrs. Ramases never touched alcohol prior to the accident. She has since learned to drink alcohol with her left hand. I am not sure if this was part of the physical therapy or a bizarre type of identification with the oppressor.

Mrs. Ramases talks frequently of her near-death experience. She goes to church three times a week and God is her companion even when she is three-sheets-to-the-wind. He is a good companion and has always been very loyal. Now, He may be leaving.

Mrs. Ramases has been an intermittent binge drinker. She has gotten stinking drunk about one time every two months for the past year and a half. She drinks only at home and never drives her car. Then she comes to us so we can punish her and hydrate her. She has not yet gone the next step to frequent binge drinking because God has been her companion. Now, He may be leaving.

Mrs. Ramases always knew before that her daughter had gone to a better place, a place that Mrs. Ramases had glimpsed before, an adumbration of immortality and rapture. Now doubt has fallen like a concrete block on Mr. Ramases' adumbration. Adumbrations are frail and do not deal well with concrete.

Mrs. Ramases needs a reconstructed adumbration. I would do this even if I did not believe in such a possibility as immortality and the joy of being one with the river. In this case, I do believe that my colleague's research is more than flawed, however. It is nice to be able to reconstruct with tools based in one's own workbox of truths.

Just because pilots experiencing oxygen loss to the brain have some of the same experiences as those momentarily held in death's waiting arms does not explain the phenomena. I have some of the same experiences as Michael Jordan playing basketball, but that does not mean I am in the same ballgame.

But there is so much more. Why would having an experience of rapture when you are close to death have any possible benefit in the evolutionary process? Why? What would make this attribute survive over time and be reproduced in successive generations? What possible edge in the war of evolution would a sensation of letting go and reaching out to the other side have in maintaining the individual gene pool? Fighting desperately against that good night should be more in keeping with sustaining the continuation of individual genes.

"Possibly it is the calm and joy that defeats shock and despair which allows the organism to survive. Could this not be the reason these individual genes are more likely to be replicated?"

Jesus, Caesar, make up your damn mind. I am trying to believe in something here. I am working on Mrs. Ramases and myself, damn it. Get a life. Besides, which do you think would have the strongest chance of evolutionary ascendency—a will to go on fighting no matter what, or a calm acceptance of the end? And does the name, Nicomedes, mean anything to you?

Why do organisms go into shock anyway? Why does all pain cease when the system is faced with terrible injury? Evolution is neither kind, nor wicked, so why would this mechanism be in place?

"All pain does not cease when some horrible trauma strikes. Sometimes death is long in coming and well sought. And Nicomedes was only a friend and ally, and long in dying."

"I do not know what to believe anymore. I was so sure, so sure," says Mrs. Ramases. Shut up, Mrs Ramases, and let me finish with Caesar for he is one of those and the good is interred with his bones.

"You must learn to accept each belief as a building block for your own reality and not demand perfect closure within the vault of logic. I accept your belief concerning the anomaly of near-death experiences, but there are an unlimited number of explanations, none of which will solve the riddle in the lotus. Pick what pleases and go on. Do not worry each possibility as if it held the solution to all others or you will spin in an endless wheel of contradictions. Accept, act and serve yourself and others for there is nothing else. All you will ever hold are the acts of kindness and beauty you give away. This is enough. Hoc opus, hic labor est." That cuts it. I am going to talk with Sulla and have you put back in charge of the vestal virgins, you sanctimonious ass.

The Weeds of God

THE STARCH IN MR. EDGARS' SAILS

Mr. Edgars has no hope. Yes, Mr. Edgars has no hope. Mr. Edgars is bereft of hope and hope is bereft of Mr. Edwards. "All this shit is useless. It's all damn useless." The world has taken the starch out of Mr. Edgars' sails. Tiny evil dwarfs with tiny little evil buckets and tiny little evil trowels have been at work taking the starch from Mr. Edgars' sails. The tiny little evil dwarfs have done their work well.

"I can't think of any reason to live if I don't have some coke to make it through the day. What is exciting to you? Is anything exciting to you? Somehow I doubt it. You don't know what it's like. You don't know how good it is. Jesus, it is wonderful. The first one is a nuclear blast of joy. I look forward to my next first one. I know, I shouldn't be actually telling the truth. I should suck up like the rest of them and tell you what you want to hear." All the tiny little evil dwarfs nod their heads and giggle. I am caught in the light and cannot flee. The deer and I await your pleasure. What is it about the light that holds us all in place? The dwarfs know, but they will not say. If I can catch one of the little buggers we will see, we will see.

"I remember the first time I did it. Jesus, I was such a jerk. I didn't know anything. It was my girl. She wanted me to try a line. I couldn't say no, I would have looked like a jerk, a real jerk. I was scared to do it. I really wanted to fake it, but she was watching me. So I thought I would just do a little to prove I was cool. I didn't know what it was going to be. I didn't even know how to do it. I watched her and I did what she did. At first it was just a numb feeling in my nose. Then, a huge door opened into a place I had never been before. It radiated through me and into the room and into her and into the walls and out into the night sky. Suddenly all the world was worthwhile. You know the feeling you get at the dentist when you are taking the nitrous oxide. That feeling that you are about to discover what the whole thing is about, why the world was put together just this way and no other, and then the feeling fades as the nitrous ends and you are sad for the shadow of truth you lost. Forget it. With coke you are just happy the whole damn thing is here, no matter why, no matter for what reason, you are just happy, happy the whole damn thing is here, happy you are here, happy herpes is here, happy warts are here, happy about puppy dogs, just happy, happy. It's better than knowing by a long shot." The little evil dwarfs are very unhappy about the knowing stuff and begin to work feverishly with their little evil trowels on Mr. Edgars' sails again.

THE SINKING OF THE INDIANAPOLIS

The water is deep. You can swim more easily in deep water. Your buoyancy is greater in deep water and no, this is not what Mark Twain means. Which will come first, the sharks or the Catalina flying boat? I am sorry we delivered the bomb. I am sorry for so many things and my heart goes out to the Japanese people. You needed oil and we would not give it unto you. We have oil here. There is a large oil slick hanging on the waves. I would give you all this oil and you would not even have to ask. I think I would prefer to decrease my buoyancy and seek shallow water, very shallow water, bathtub water. I want to invite everyone over for a bath, but I do not think I will ever be clean again.

"I don't want to have affairs. Sometimes you can't help it. I want them when I see them. It seems so easy and what is the damn big deal? I don't love them, I just want them. Jesus, you would think I had killed someone the way she acts. I told her it didn't mean anything. Then she says what if she did it, but it's not the same thing. She was just saying it. She doesn't really want someone else. I take care of business at home too if you know what I mean. She is happy with it. She doesn't want anybody else. I really want them. That's different. I love my wife, but I have to have some kind of diversion. You understand. I know you have the same feelings. I know you aren't married because someone told me, but I know you have the same feelings because every man does. That's just the way it is." Mr. Edmonds looks at his hands as if confirmation was written in the lines of his palm. I wonder if we will ever get home. I have never been so cold. I can hear screams, many screams. We are sprinkled in the ocean like corks. We bob and sink for we are bait in this painted ocean waiting, waiting. I dream of the sound of engines droning in the distance. All has failed us except the oil and the sharks who coat us with their random possibilities.

I never seem to get all the dirt out from underneath my fingernails. Why is this? Is this a genetic possibility? Do all the Irish keep a little of the old sod beneath their fingernails no matter where they may be? Did Bobby Burns have dirt beneath his fingernails? Did *Auld Lang Syne* refer to dirt from days gone by?

SOME TRUTHS BETTER LEFT UNTURNED

Name some reasons not to die: rum and coke, country ham and biscuits, Joseph Heller, running alone in the woods with snow falling, the sound of rain on a tin roof, the sight and smell of the ocean, walking a trail through woods that climb toward the unseen sky, knowing you have actually helped someone while risking something you valued, knowing you have maintained your integrity even at great cost, allowing those who have harmed you to retire with dignity when you could give great harm, the love of a large, ugly dog who asks nothing and gives all, the sights and smells of a walk in summer's fields, and finishing with honor. I love hokey. I just love the damn stuff. Sometimes I think it is all worthwhile, but I would not do it over again. No, I would not do it over again even if I could change it all I wished. I feel I have paid once and I do not want to run the course again. I have gotten all the way to here, and I will not go back. No, I will not go back no matter where here gets to be.

"I think when your time is spent, you will wish to go back. Even Brutus would wish to go back. Yes, I do think of him. You were right, but for all the wrong reasons. You have that kind of luck. Did you know?"

Yes Caesar, I know. I have been told before. Will you take some wine now that you denied yourself before? No, well it continues then. You still fear losing control. You fear what you will see and what others will see of you.

"That is true, but that is not why I refuse the cup. It gives me no pleasure. That is why I refuse. I do not share your desire to seek all that confuses and confounds."

I like the wine, Caesar. I like the process of drinking my mind into new places. I like the swirls of memory and the new turns of phrase and thought it affords. I like to watch as others begin to reach into parts of their minds unnoticed by sobriety and share these little wonderments with their fellows.

"You speak falsely, but then you know that too and there are some truths better left unturned."

GENERAL STAFFING AND THE BIG KAHUNA

It is general staffing and we are discussing things untoward on our units. Everyone is happy to be here and the Cyclone "B" tablets are suspended in the drop ceiling. "I cannot cover every damn thing on this unit for the paltry sum I am getting from the damn state and that's a damn fact and I am tired of it. Charting, charting, charting. Every time I damn well turn around some damn nurse is calling about something not being in the chart. I am damn tired of it. Damn tired." Dr. Monttous is damn tired. I am damn tired. We are all damn tired in this place.

"Those asses at state have the brains of pigeons. Let those damn bureaucrats get a medical degree before they try to tell me how to treat patients. We need at least two more psychiatrists to cover this damn unit." Marat applauds along with all the other Jacobins. Charlotte lovingly caresses Dr. Monttous' blond hair. "This man needs a bath."

"I am also damn tired of some damn nurse calling me in the middle of the damn night to tell me that some damn patient needs some damn thing right now and it can't wait tell morning. Jesus, you would think everything around here is a damn crisis. How many crises can one damn little unit have? This shit has got to stop." In the distance the shit stops, but only for a stunned minute and rolls on.

"Do any of you get the picture? Let's carry our own weight and stop expecting the damn physicians to do all the work. Is that clear? Can you even understand what I am saying?" New sects are rapidly formed advocating a return to the tower of Babel. Let's build that puppy higher this time and see what the consequences could be.

"Jesus, are you people painted on the walls? Some of you other physicians should at least have the same feelings. What is wrong with you people?" Some of the other physicians wake up momentarily, but they have been up all night answering calls from the damn nurses and quickly return to slumber. Charlotte nods wisely and blows a kiss to Dr. Monttous.

"We don't even have a damn union. Even the nurses have a damn union. If I represented the clinical staff here, I would make some damn changes and that's for damn sure."

Dr. Willibun hangs up the telephone on which he has been having a very important conversation that none of the rest of us are important enough to know about. "Thank you, Dr. Monttous, for your comments. I shall go on with my appointed rounds with a lighter heart. In the meantime, I have decided to place you on the on-call list for the next thirty days so you can study the issue. Please entertain me with a full report next month. Make that a full report in writing and send it to my secretary." The big kahuna has spoken and the room rings with applause.

SHOOTING MR. LANDSBE

I am lonely. Time seems to be held in a vise. Mr. Landsbe is revealing his thoughts on the origins of the universe. We are just getting to the cooling of large gaseous masses.

One and one half billion years ago we diverged from plants. Mr. Landsbe proves this was a mistake. The potted plants in the window are slowly dying during his dissertation. They long for the fields of winter where his voice is absent. Yet, he is a constant reminder they chose well.

"I had a good time when I was in college. It was a good time. I really did very well. I had a lot of friends and good times. I mean those were good times. That's where I met my wife. Yes, it was in the spring of 1987. I know I told you this before, but there are some things I want to go over. Look at them in a new light. That's what this is all about, right?"

Two of the geraniums have wrapped themselves together attempting to squeeze themselves to death. I get up and pull both of them out by the roots. Do dead geraniums dream?

I have tried to direct Mr. Landsbe towards more meaningful topics. I have tried for twenty-six years and forty-five minutes. All attempts have failed. We are down to three bullets and the water has run out. We await further instructions and shall remain at our posts.

"I don't know what college was like for you, but I really enjoyed it. I was the head of my frat. I was really a BMOC in those days. Patty was the homecoming queen. She was beautiful then; not fat at all. Everyone wanted her. I was really something in those days. I remember when . . . "

I put the geraniums back in the pot. If I can endure it, they can endure it. The hands of the clock have stopped moving. They long to return to the Bulova factory where Mr. Landsbe never speaks because no one from the frat goes there.

I open my right hand drawer and pull out a Colt 1911. I get up and walk comely to the side of Mr. Landsbe's chair and place the muzzle of the gun against his temple.

"I am just going to say this once, so listen very, very carefully. If you do not start dealing with your problem, if you do not start discussing what is really troubling you, and if you continue speaking never ending dribble I am going to blow a large hole in the side of your head. Then the geraniums and I will look inside your head with a flashlight to see if we can find the problem." The geraniums have grown two inches and the hands on the clock begin to move because they know who I am going to shoot.

DYING ON FRIDAY

"Do you realize that there are beings who can see the electromagnetic currents that surrounds us? Is their reality any more real than those like you who are oblivious to the web of energy that is woven around you?

There is an infinite number of realities, not one of which is more or less real than another. You are appalled at the horror, despair, humiliation, ignorance, madness, inequity, and futility that pervades your reality. There is no more truth in your thoughts than there is in the reality of birds navigating within a rainbow tunnel of photon macadam.

Hold! Do not speak, but listen to your own thoughts and that which you seek so much. It is death that you most fear, no matter what else you speak. You fear it will end before you can make sense of it, before you can requite the wrongs that pile up around you. This is what you fear most. You desperately wish to know what it all means, and above all you wish the time, time above all, to know."

You are truly an ass, Caesar, you who acted always in your own best interest. Christ, give it a break.

"Of course I acted in my own interest. How could I have acted otherwise? Whatever I do, whatever I decide to do, must be in what I perceive as my own best interest, or I would not act so. Neutrinos act in their own best interest, quarks act in their own best interest, all act within their own best interest. All of what you call energy and matter act within their own best interest and none is more or less alive to the possibility than another.

Is an elephant more alive than a virus or a planet less alive than a sun? There is an interlocking infinity of Mobius systems of being pulsating within an infinity of dimensions. And it is never-ending and always balanced because there is no other possibility. There is an infinite balance in which no line can be rewritten and no line can be changed.

Yet each minute possibility can be altered an infinite number of times for each time is an infinite number of dimensions. Nothing will alter the outcome because there is none to alter.

Wait! You have screamed for the answer, then now listen to it. We are the outcomes. You can no more cease than matter or energy can cease. You have been and will be. Your cessation would end the equation, but you are not the sum of today nor the sum of all your yesterdays or tomorrows. You are no more the child who had no answer to Mrs. Baths' math question and died on Friday, than you are the psychologist who seeks answers to questions having no possibility of closure. It is not a question of knowing all possibilities for it is all possibilities that is the God you seek. It is not a possibility of being with the force or against the force, or following the way or not following the way. It is a matter written in the details for you have only details to change. Details are the building blocks of energy that make this fulcrum of possibilities.

Each day you have the possibility of changing the details. Every decision is a microcosm of all change, an instant when time and dimensions can be changed within an infinity of dimensions and time. This is your glory and despair for we are one in God.

You will kill yourself on a Friday not too far and for "no apparent reason." You can, however, no more stop all being than you can stop your being. It does not start over again because it never ends, but you will have emptied this possibility and another will be extended."

God, you are an ass. You write well in Latin, and to your great credit, you fought well in Latin, but you forget that dying on Friday does no better in Latin than English. You ass.

The Weeds of God

THE DOG IN THE WINDOW

Mr. Stils has watched the window for ten minutes. Nothing has happened in the window, or , at least, I have seen nothing happening in the window. I wish I could see what Mr. Stils sees in the window.

"I do not know why I feel so sad. I need a drink, but I do not think that is the reason I feel sad. I've got lots of money and what most people would believe is a good life, but I really don't give a damn. I do give a lot to charities and they seem to love me for it even though I give strategically to limit my taxes and deliberately pick stupid causes to support. I give to the Sierra Club even though they have become an irrational pack of dirt lovers. I am afraid they may find out that the polio virus is on the endangered species list and fight to bring it back. I wonder why I said that." We return to the window.

"Maybe I am like the polio virus, just a stone's throw from being extinct. I do not know why I would want to keep going. In fact, I don't know if I want to keep going. Why do you want to keep going? No, I know you won't answer. Strangely enough I would like to know what you really think. Come to think of it, I would like to know what anyone would really think. They think, therefore I am." We return to the window.

"I am. I am desperate for something to do that means something. I make money and it seems so easy. Maybe if I was desperate for food I would feel differently. It is all relative. I hate most of my relatives. No, I don't hate them, I just don't care one way or the other. They all act like I am wonderful because I have a lot of money and can do things for them and their boring children. That's why most people like me. There is no me, only my money is me. I am money. I know I'm not good looking, but my money is good looking. I know my wife shows off my money and not me when she takes me to a party. She wants them to see all the money she has on her arm, the little monkey with all the money that he made all by himself after dropping out of college. Actually I liked the college. It was a pretty good time. There was a girl who might have loved me. She was ugly like me, but she might have loved me. I have an ugly dog that loves me. Strange, the only thing I really miss is that old dog. I know the dog is waiting by the door for me. I don't think anyone else is waiting at the door." We return to the window and the dog who waits patiently by the door.

MR. RUNLUTTER'S SENSE OF PROPORTION

"I hate this damn place. We don't do anything. The groups are a crock and these sessions are meaningless. I am hurting. I need something to stop the hurting. You don't have any idea what I am going through. Your lousy Sinequan detox regimen is useless. I need something today. I need something. You can at least do that. I can't talk to you until I can feel better." Mr. Runlutter is smoking a carton of Kools. He has a hose hooked up to the carton which is smouldering in the trash can. Mr. Runletter is withdrawing from heroin and heroin is withdrawing from Mr. Runletter.

"Do you know how good the damn stuff makes you feel? I can taste the sound of good times in my mind. Shit. You can't believe how good it is. I still remember the first time. God, it was fantastic. You always look for that first time again. I know I will go right back to it as soon as I can get out of here. You can write that down. I don't care. The judge is going to crucify my ass anyway. My stupid lawyer thinks I can get off with just the time I will spend in here, but I know the judge will get me. I'll do five years this time. If I had killed somebody I would do seven years. Seems just a little unjust. There is something wrong with this country's sense of proportion." The judge walks in to look at Mr. Runletter. He takes Mr. Runletter's Sinequan meds and steals the carton of Kools. His robes are very black and he has a white shirt on. He goes to church every Sunday and seldom commits adultery. He has a large black dog named Stout. His wife likes the fact that he is a judge. She likes the fact that his mind is slow and ponderous and easily manipulated. She is very comfortable, but sometimes she thinks life might hold other possibilities. It could be.

"What is all this about? If I want to do drugs, who cares? Who is hurt besides me? Jesus, it's my damn business. I'm not hurting anyone but me. Right? There is supposed to be a separation of church and state. Is taking drugs a sin? Why should it be illegal? Why should I do the same amount of time for drugs as manslaughter? This is crazy. Just legalize the shit and you would stop all the crooks. Look at prohibition. All those people killed for nothing. Alcohol is still a worse drug than heroin. Jesus, heroin wouldn't be worth ten dollars a pound if it was legalized. No one would be interested in selling it except the government. Is everybody crazy? But then you wouldn't have a job. Right?" Mr. Runletter is looking at the scales of justice. He has found the weights hidden underneath. This woman has been snorting cocaine. She is doing a blind quality assurance check for a Columbian cartel.

SONGS

What is this thing called love? Songs have been running forcefully through my mind today. They just pop up and have their way with the screen where messages are posted. I wonder who sets the screen up and who decides on what messages will be accepted. I wonder. "Fallen trees and Wounded Knee. Stars that die at dawn and curling fangs upon the fawn."

"I am feeling much better. I mean, I don't hurt like I was hurting. Jesus, it is one lousy feeling. You would think it would be enough to stop you from doing it again, but mostly I thought how great a drink would be. I mean, that's what I thought, but I knew it was wrong, but I thought it just the same. Yes, I thought it just the same. Has my wife called about me? No, I asked the nurse and she said no. I don't know why I asked you that. I'm still a little messed up I guess." Mr. Jest looks at the pictures on the wall and avoids eye contact. Psychomotor agitation is present. I avoid eye contact and pat my foot on the floor hidden from Mr. Jest by my made-at-the-state-pen desk.

"I don't know why I want to drink. It just seems to start. When I am feeling really great, I want to go out and celebrate and when I am feeling really bad I want to feel a little better and forget. I guess that's why. I mean, maybe I really have always known why. I guess that's it really in a nutshell." Mr. Jest looks at the nutshell in his hand. He turns it over and over. Two squirrels bang on the window and shake their heads. They are holding a tiny sign. One is pointing to it. "I guess that's it in a hamburger." Mr. Jest ignores them. They make another sign and depart.

"My wife is the nicest person I know. She is very nice. You've met her. Yes, she is very nice and she said she liked you." Mr. Jest looks at the nutshell. "Do you think I will ever stop drinking?"

"I think you can stop drinking, Mr. Jest. I also think something is troubling you more than just the fact that your wife is a nice person." I read my cognitive re-engineering manual to make sure I have said this just right. Yep, right on the money.

"You asked me if I slept well at night, if I had any physical complaints, if I had any significant weight gains or losses in the past six months, if I had headaches, if I had any problems with vision, if my processes of elimination had changed, if I had thoughts that I couldn't seem to stop from running through my mind, if I ever thought of suicide, if I ever thought of just running away and a lot of other things designed to see if I am depressed. I told you no. I mean, I said no." It don't mean a thing if it ain't got that swing. My processes of elimination are changing and not for the better.

"I had a normal childhood. I like my parents." I had a normal childhood and I like Mr. Jest's parents. I am going nowhere and I am taking Mr. Jest with me. I'll be around when he's gone, and just now and then, drop a line to say you're feeling fine. Just now and then.

The Weeds of God

GOYA'S DOG

I hate Goya. He lived in a sea of despair in a small submarine with many large leaks. I hate the *Drowning Dog* for I have seen it all my life. I hate Goya for painting this and for what he saw and most of all, for demanding that others at least pay momentary attention to it.

Goya would paint Mr. Livingston. He would paint him many times. And, some day I will kill him for doing just this and no more.

"I can't count the number of times I have let people down. My wife is a much better counter. She can tell you the exact number; each of them has a large file with annotations and cross references. My wife is a CPA for failure. She, of course, married just the right man for such a position. To be more honest, possibly she developed the expertise from being in the company of the possibilities." Mr. Livingston pulls out his copy of the *Drowning Dog* and writes a small annotation on the corner.

Mr. Livingston looks much like the *Drowning Dog*. I have thrown him as many lifelines as I can, but we are both drowning, he and I.

"I feel like killing myself virtually every day of my life when I'm sober. Strange, when I have had just the right amount of alcohol I feel like the world is a very happy place indeed. I like talking with people and I think I am very witty and kind. I think most people are very witty and kind when I have just the right amount. I have always been more somber than my fellows even as a child. You admitted that some people are genetically more prone to sadness and depression. I am that person. I feel the sadness around me more than others, and I do not understand how they cannot feel it too, or maybe, they just hide it better than I."

Yes, you are right Mr. Livingston, some are born to hear more clearly the cries of despair that surround them. Each cry causes another wave to form within the drowning sea. You send more waves over me, Mr. Livingston, and even Goya despairs.

The most moving songs and poems are of sadness and despair for they are so much easier to share and all have the ring of truth. Joy is too easily envied by those who do not share it.

"Why would it be of any benefit in the accident of evolution to have a predilection to melancholy? Do people bond more readily with those who do not appear happy? Do we fear those who are always filled with happiness and bounce around through the world like kittens finding their first large ball of yarn to unravel? Maybe, I am just someone who came into the world having already unraveled the ball and found what is at the end of the string."

I LOVE YOU MR. HAMSUNG

Rommel drives on toward Hanoi. Clouds of sand mark the panzer's course, and Montgomery is just another chicken for the pot. The Hated-Cong weave blankets on Navajo reservations in Arizona longing for rice paddies and the smell of the sea. Nothing will be the same again.

I love you, Mr. Hamsung. I love your honesty and your misunderstandings. I love your willingness to stay on the hill no matter what they threw at you. I love you Mr. Hamsung and I am desperate to help, but alas desperation is not enough.

I want to hold you in my heart and tell you all is well. I want you to see yourself and what you can be. I want to help you let go of what no longer can be held. I want you to keep the beauty you have wrought and cast aside the demons that found you. You can make up all the rest if only you will see, but I cannot seem to give light to the far corners where the demons hide.

"I remember so many people who won't come this way again. All the beautiful things die and assholes are cultured in petri dishes the size of California. Its alright, I know I've lost her. You know, you were right. I really held on to her just because I wanted something that had not faded and died. The person I remember never existed, or I saw differently then, or some prism through which I looked has been broken. I know, the reason makes no difference only the reality. I believe you, at least sometimes I believe you. Maybe I just need to believe somebody and you are the least harmful possibility. You want the truth or whatever I can find of it? I would rather go back, go back to my make-believe-love. I would like to have the privilege of my own gentle lies. I do not want this new bright light. I wish to go home again. I want everything to be very, very comfortable and fit the contours of my mind. I don't want things that stick out, parts of a puzzle I do not remember. I want to go home." The Hated-Cong have paused in the endless weaving of already discarded rugs. Nothing will be the same again. There is no home to go back to and there is no beginning to cherish or abhor.

I have tried to take threads from the weave and help you put them back in a pattern you can hold, a pattern that leads to a different future and different choices. But then, what the hell do I know? I cannot really see all the threads, only through your mind darkly and my mind darkly and my mind grows darker with the passing of your days. Could Rommel sing the blues and did he hope for shower shoes and look forward to new movies with Jerry Lewis and buttered popcorn and hula-hoops and knowing that James Mason would make him immortal? There is no home to go back to?

UNANIMOUS DECISIONS

We are about to have our monthly executive staff meeting. These are always a joy. I virtually live from one to the next. Each meeting is a stepping stone to nirvana. It is considered a great privilege to be welcomed to the group. All the real decisions concerning the unit are made in these meetings and all the other meetings are window dressings of kindness to the peasants who do all the work on the unit. I love this. This is democracy at work. God, I love this place.

Four of us sit in the conference room. We arrived in relation to our positions on the table of hierarchal insignificance. I arrived first and five minutes before the scheduled meeting. I was alone with adversity. Soon Dr. Bibly and Dr. Krieg arrived together because neither of them can form a complete sentence without the other. Five minutes later came Mr. Edgars. Mr. Edgars launched into a discussion of the therapeutic benefits of playing tennis. Everyone agreed. Later the door burst open and two acolytes rushed in to throw themselves face down on the floor. They were covered with rose petals. Dr. Mondriatus entered with a great rush of speed, his white lab coat trying valiantly to keep up with him as it made a cape in the wind of his passing. "Why do they always do that?" asked Dr. Mondriatus. "I do like those rose petals. That's a nice touch."

"Let's get down to it. Everybody has interviewed all the candidates for the new psychiatrist position and we've gone over their credentials. Let's have some discussion on who to choose, " states Dr. Mondriatus as he looks through his latest copy of Penthouse.

"I think there is really only one choice, Dr. Vigilius Ghondrobowski," states Mr. Edgars. "He meets every requirement and then some and he plays a mean game of tennis." Mr. Edgars returns to stringing a new tennis racquet.

"Well, if that's it, we can all agree on Dr. Ghondrobowski," states Dr. Mondriatus and shows the centerfold to the assembly. Each of us signs his initials on Miss December.

I ponder if this is worth the wasted effort. I ponder Miss December. "Dr.Mondriatus, do you not think there are two, or three, or all of the other candidates who are more qualified. Dr. Ghondrobowski, while undoubtedly the best tennis player, did his residency at Dumpers State Hospital which is about equivalent to having completed one at Walgreens. His medical degree was obtained in Poland under a communist regime that has conviently lost all of his records and he does not even have a wart."

"Of course his medical degree was obtained in Poland, he's Polish. I love his dialect. I can barely understand a damn thing he says. He does speak perfect French, however, and what is wrong with Dumpers? Nothing is wrong with Dumpers. It has passed federal inspection every year, and I can tell you that is amazing as hell. The quality of service in that place is just above Dachau. That means the psychiatrists must be nearly perfect for it to pass every year. Damned amazing," states Mr. Edgars as he adds a few more pounds of tension to his strings.

"Possibly everyone has forgotten that Dr. Ghondrowboski was unable to correctly diagnosis even a single one of the patients' charts which he reviewed. He also can barely understand or communicate with the majority of our patients or staff. This would seem to be somewhat of a drawback to functioning at maximum efficiency. Wait, I may need to rethink that concept." I again initial Miss December.

"I don't think that anyone can deny that Dr. Ghondrobowski is the nephew of the Commissioner of Mental Health. In fact, I defy anyone to bring such a charge against Dr. Ghondrobowski and that is the crux of the argument," states Mr. Edgars.

"Wait. This is getting out of hand and everything should be within hand around here or I'm not the Hierophant of Eleusis. It doesn't have anything to do with his being the nephew of the Commissioneer. He's a fine physician and that's all she wrote on the matter. I have decided that we all agree that Dr. Ghondrobowski is the choice. I don't think it

The Weeds of God

could be any more democratic even though the final decision is mine and mine alone. Does anyone believe otherwise? No. This is democracy at work. Dr. Ghondrobowski is our unanimous choice. I think we can say that unanimously. I think we can also get the Commissioner to rethink his decision on our secondary funding for the unit. The two are not connected and no one should think otherwise. I think we cannot think otherwise unanimously. We are as unanimous as unanimous can be," states Dr. Mondriatus.

SHE THAT HER OWN HAND SLEW

My eyes hurt. This is the only form of a hangover I ever get. The gods hate me. No matter how long I drink, there seems to be no next day physical sanction. There are many other sanctions, however. I have to try to make small talk and be charming with women I do not remember who will not notice my passing any more than I will. We have to act out the rest of the play as a matter of good manners. I wonder if she was thinking the same thoughts and wondering why we could not just both gently disappear? Did we both fear saying something clumsy in our haste to be rid of the other's presence? It is like looking at the mess after a meal. No matter how lovely the meal, the remains are not appealing. We were new and interesting for a while, like a place unknown that we visited. All our old stories that had been said and died came back to life for this new audience. The best material dies quickly in morning's light.

I never eat breakfast and I never trust a man who does. A Coke and a cigarette are the components of a good breakfast for a gentleman. Thoughts begin to come loose that have been captured in the net of dreams. They can be mulled over, sorted and polished. This is best done alone. I sit at the table with cigarette smoke hanging from the ceiling. There are many thoughts laying on the table. One of them is the death of Dr. Tilenon. Dr. Tilenon is dead, she that her own hand slew who lies unburied at crossroads of thoughts all blue.

She ingested massive amounts of aspirin and bled to death. All alone she bled to death. She was short and fat and did not speak well and she had been bleeding to death for many years. Dr. Tilenon had been taking drugs for years, but many denied that she possessed such imagination. I did not enjoy Dr. Tilenon. She started every conversational gambit with a defensive move. I understood, but still could not help. I feared what would come of trying although I did try in the long ago beginning. Yes, I remember that I did try, but I did not try to continue.

She feared rejection in remembrance of all such times past. She was safe only with her patients, and even then there was always their hidden thoughts. Fearing what would be, she insured she struck first to let you know she did not care and would fight if cornered. A hiss from the cat who lives in the corner with the maimed leg dragging, always dragging behind it and she was gone.

I could have done so much more. She died choked in her own blood. She died in great and terrible pain. Is this the pain she wished to give to all those who had given her such pain? I could have tried a million times more than I did. I could have discussed artichokes and Mark Twain's references to the Upanishads hidden in *The Adventures of Huckleberry Finn*. I could have admitted that I am scared most of the time. I could have admitted that I have seen an angel, not a large angel, but definitely an angel.

No one invited her anywhere because they were mostly as scared of her as she was of them. Everyone feared what she would say and the lash of her words against them. I feared her too, and I let her die. Even in death she did not invite anyone. She died alone. She died giving the most pain her mind could conceive. Everyone will come to the funeral for at last she is one of us.

THE FLAVOR OF QUARKS

I have been reading about supersymmetry and drinking rum and cokes. The rum has helped a lot. I am amazed that so few members of the species have the slightest idea about the building blocks of the world in which they live. In all the world only a very few physicists have the vaguest notion of the strings that bind it all together and still it goes on. I am an idiot for such things and a Vegan to boot. Larangian density and Yukawa interactions be damned. None of this explains the interactions of rum and coke.

I look at the formulas on the page and watch my gerbil as he explores the intricate universe of his wheel. Does he know the Seldon plan? Has he realized the infinity of the wheel of samsara? Does he know there is no reason the quadratic polynomial should respect, or even give a damn about, degeneracy among slepton masses? This world is full of degeneracy. Here at least is something I can speak to with great knowledge.

Tell me, Caesar, did you feel small when Sosigenes gave you sixty-seven days? That is small in comparison to bosuns and flavors and dark matter.

"You constantly seek what you already posses and deny what you already believe," states Caesar and autographs a copy of one of my Classics Illustrated comics. I already posses bosuns and flavor and dark matter? Could I patent those babies and live happily ever after or what.

"You must believe most of all in belief, for every fact casts another shadow of inevitable demand for an ultimate fact. Every new explanation only creates the need for a new explanation. No matter how deep you search beneath the atom and the forces that hold space, energy, and mass in time, there appears yet another ripple beneath the wave." My gerbil stops and looks at Caesar, but soon returns to his appointed rounds.

TO HELL WITH PSYCHOMETRICS

It is raining heavily. I like the rain. As I grow older, I like the rain more and more. It brings a curtain of isolation to my world. I somehow feel safer in the rain. It becomes more difficult for anything to intrude.

Dr. Ellis is intruding. Dr. Ellis is explaining why we do not need psychometrics for every patient. It is a waste of time according to Dr. Ellis, who is also a waste of time. "A real doctor gets his information from knowing what to ask and what to look for in the patient's behavior. You do not need all the garbage involved in testing procedures based on some lab rat's repertoire. This is more than some lab test. You must feel what the patient feels, that is the essence of the process." Dr. Ellis smooths a fold in his ermine robe and picks his teeth with an ivory splinter from his elephant tusk. Cows moo in the distant contented to be milked again and Britain will be saved by Diocletian only to find that he persecuted Christians.

I am lost in the argument. Should I speak of the Rorschach electric? Should I tell of the tossing of the runes? Must such things be revealed to this unlearned shit? The quantum theory of psychometrics should not be given to the layman lest they pervert it to their own ends.

"I could not agree with you more, Dr. Ellis. I can think of no way to agree with you more than I presently do and that is the truth. You can see it in my behavior and you can feel it in your soul and that is a fact. To hell with psychometrics, let us reach into their souls. By the way, have you ever had a Rorschach? No, well I have a set of the large cards that you might enjoy."

"Your supposed wit grates from time to time. Take some advice, and just do what you are asked. As yet, you do not run this place." Dr. Ellis has armed himself in this battle of wits. He is usually suicidal in these instances. Why am I such a petty jerk? He has his right to his opinion and he is even right from time to time. Even then, however, he manages to be all wrong about it. He is condescending to all his patients and most of them love him for it. They do not even know how scared he is of them. Why should they? It would not help. He does see all his patients and he does seem to try. Why am I so damn petty and why do I look forward to being in charge of the place so I can have Dr. Ellis charged with crimes against humanity and make him wear funny hats? Sadly I know the answer to these questions. I must try to forget these answers and simply enjoy the opportunities Dr. Ellis presents. Yes, I must learn to revel in pettiness so that I can be worthy of being in charge of this place. I must be true to myself, but I must stop making up imaginary patients and sticking them in Dr. Ellis' assignment folder and watching in wonder as he looks around the unit for Mr. S. Mallmind and Mr. Al Coholic. How can I hope for a better world unless I am willing to contribute?

THE CLOG-DANCING SHIVA

There are at least ten dimensions, but time is not one of these, only a frivolity of relativities conjured by other aspiring dimensions. Of what does gravity dream, and what makes it decide to curve space, and why does space comply? Five years have passed since the Word Trade Center was struck. Yet I remember only weeks, weeks of small numbers passing. So many times it is like this, time seems to lie, to falsify, disown and vilify my own beliefs as if they were the meanderings of a patient's mind.

I have turned momentarily to the mirror and found myself a year older, yet I have known years to pass when the clock shows only hours have fallen to its hand. Damn the bosuns of time who refuse to follow the rules of the macrocosmic kingdom above, beyond, below or where? Is there hope in this abysmal confusion?

It is my birthday within the ides of March where you too Caesar fell. I am thirty-five and spelling macular degeneration and the futile protests of dying neurons finding death across the blood-brain barrier where none go without a coin for Charon and a smile for Nike's loss. I am thirty-five and at last passing out of adolescence. It is not a good feeling. What many funny things do I have left to be or not to be? I would not go back and start again. It seems unfathomable that anyone would wish to start again. I am headed towards some destination I have ordained and I do not wish to go back for I would lose the distance I have already traveled. I would look young again if I did not have to pay the price of all my time lived over.

I think everyone lives the same length of time. If you live a year or a hundred years it is the same. The billions of events happening within the universe of infinite possibilities are clipped each moment from time, falling on to the barbershop floor of the past. The pain and suffering, the joy and glory of yesterday are spent and cannot be played again. Possibly only the acts of kindness you give away are capable of enduring time's maw. I sing to you of the Clog-Dancing Shiva and of events never having unfolded within time's realm. Does

Shiva get athlete's foot and does Amaterasu use sunscreen to protect her from herself?

"You are wandering in your own desire to despair. I would, however, agree with the irrelevance of time."

The earth is tilted at approximately 23.5%. Does it enjoy this approximately? Is this the perfect tilt, just so to lure into its proximity other possibilities and shun those not so well loved? Is there here some unrequited love affair with Haley's comet?

"I don't know if I can kick this stuff. You must hear the same thing all the time. But, I really don't know if I can kick it. Codeine makes me feel so good. Life just rolls by me and I am happy; no matter what happens I am happy. There is a rainbow in my mind when I am on the stuff. I have a secret life that is a cave from which I can watch the others pass by. I like having the secret. It makes me feel very safe and comfortable and . . . somehow removed from all the madness around me. I am so damn cool when she is there," says Mr. Beem and I know he is right. Mr. Beem is a tall handsome man with a James Dean shyness that stumbles around a room and makes everyone else very comfortable. He is also a fourth degree black belt in Karate, but he never suggests the possibility. Dr. Grite, who also is a fourth degree black belt and wears a neon sign to that effect, told me and swore me to secrecy with the secret handshake . . . the one that will break your fingers if you are not very clever.

"I like taking the first pill in the morning. I know that the effects will begin in about twenty minutes. It slowly slips into your mind like a large gentle cat with great claws, and purrs ripple through your mind like endless waves upon a crescent beach. I like waiting, knowing that soon the waves will begin to touch me and build slowly to put my mind at ease. Behind the bar with his mind at ease, behind the bar with his mind at ease." I know Mr. Beem, behind the bar with your mind at ease. I know. All of us want it so.

"I wish there was some other way to do it that did not involve so many problems, but I fear there is none. No, I know that I must pay and I know that I take a great chance each time, but somehow that adds to the magic. I am in a secret society of one and I do not want anyone else to join. Sometimes I read a book that I love so much, I want no one else to ever read it. That is very selfish, but it is true. If everyone had this magic, what would the magic be? Part of the joy is looking on with the knowledge that you are beyond the limits of others, and in a place they do not know. I like that." Mr. Beem is a tiger in a night of burning bright and he has no need for stinking symmetry.

"When the lady leaves, I feel an explosion of sadness that bursts in my mind. I claw the walls inside of me, scratching and snarling to find her again. I fear what I would do to get her back." I love you so, Mr. Beem, and I have told you true. Soon the chipping that you do, the few pills a day to bring the lady, will not be enough to lure her to your side. She will ask so much more, and, I fear, you will pay. The ten days you spend with us will only make your heart grow fonder still, but she will not be yours at so small a price for long. You will walk the Street Without Joy to find her this time, and she will come to you again, and take from you the gentleness that will fall away. I will miss you Mr. Beem, behind the bar with your mind at ease.

ANAL RETENTIVES

What is the meaning of this? I love that question. Few people can really deliver this question well. Winston Churchill could do it, but Dr. Boethius pales in comparison. When Dr. Boethius asks the question, you really feel like he may be referring to the adjective. That is why I responded with, "being the person, thing or idea that is present."

When Churchill was notified that the Italians had entered the war on the side of the Axis powers, he responded, "It is only fair, we had them last time." That is the way I feel about Dr. Boethius although we have him this time, and no one is more fun in staffing than this prince of a fellow.

Dr. Boethius was upset with one of my chart notes which read, "Patient's wife has refused to have sex with him for past five months and, consequently, he has taken the matter into his own hand." The meaning is clear in my opinion. Dr. Boethius believes that this is a flippant remark that has no place in the patient's chart. I believe there could be no better place for it, and I have looked for many places to put it.

The conversational gamuts were interrupted when Mr. Willnon started screaming in room 2B. Dr. Boethius immediately questioned, "What is that?" I of course replied, "A function word to introduce a noun clause that is usually the subject or object of the verb or the predicate nominative." Before Dr. Boethius could question the predicate nominative, Nurse Edwads screamed too and off went Dr.Boethius. I must get some tapes of screams to play on call. They are incredibly effective around here.

Nurse Jones rushes in all breathless to state, "He is throwing feces all over the damn walls." I stop to assure Nurse Jones that I am sure Dr. Boethius has his reasons for this behavior and that he is probably suffering from predicate nominative syndrome with multiple complications. Nurse Jones asks, "What are we going to do?" "Remember, Nurse Jones, that even Dr. Boethius has a limited amount of this type of ammunition, so I suggest that we just wait him out." This, of course, is my suggested course of action for all behavior on the unit.

I make a mental note to pick up a bag of fresh manure from the zoo to present to Mr. Willnon in his next session. Dr.Boethius should be happy with this as he claims Mr. Willnon is an anal retentive, and surely nothing could give more credence to his concepts than being faced with Mr. Willnon and a full bag of manure. This way both of them will come to the contest equally armed.

MY GRANDFATHER WAS A GIANT

I have a picture of my grandfather on my desk. He is standing next to an old pot-bellied stove in a house far, far away. It is early morning and he has just started the fire in the pot-bellied stove. The stove is very happy and I am very happy. Grandfather has the slightest of smiles and it is reflected in the pot-bellied stove. Usually my grandfather had that smile. He was much amused by the world around him. He gave it a lot and he expected a lot from it. My grandfather was a giant. Sometimes I look into the picture and feel myself falling back in time to that warm moment beside the pot-bellied stove and my grandfather's smile. I remember that moment with clarity and love, but it cannot be held forever.

I remember holding his hand in the hospital bed as he died. He said goodbye and smiled, and the pot-bellied stove smiled and welcomed him home. Slowly, like a bright light fading gently into darkness, he disappeared into the hospital bed and he has not been seen again. There are many rumors of him and the pot-bellied stove, but they have not been seen again. There are many rumors. There are many rumors of him and the pot-bellied stove, like a faint wind gently teasing the curtains in the windows of my mind.

My grandfather was a giant
He was as tall as a summer sky
He was the sound of laughter
And childhood when it died

He was Easter and turkey
And Christmas and toys
He was John Wesley Harding
And the Dalton boys

He was so much more
Than I could hope to be
Lord I loved him so
He was everything to me

He is sleeping in the shadows
That play around the hill
Where the grass is quiet and soft
And the wind is always still

There is an angel on a tombstone
Who stoops as if to hear
The laughter in the voice
Of the giant who sleeps here

Come take my hand and guide me
It seems I have lost my way
Is there anything to live for
Must I face another day

When the world become too much
And every color is blue
I remember the giant
who sleeps beneath the dew

The Weeds of God

EMERGENT COMPUTERS OF GOD

Mr. Ticks is snoring. Should I wake him? No. I can sleep through the rest of the session with Mr. Ticks and we will both be the better for it. Sleep heals all wounds.

"I am not sleeping. I am thinking, Grasshopper. Are we not all emergent computers? Plants and animals - maybe rocks and dirt - are all just emergent computers. Einstein was an emergent computer, albeit a hell of a model. You are just an emergent computer even though you think you talk with Caesar. Yes, I know about that. Baffling is it not?"

I know that Mr. Ticks does not know about Caesar, or at least, he does not know I talk with him when I am drunk, and, even sometimes when I am not. I was coming out of my therapeutic coma and imaging either what Mr. Ticks said or what I heard. That is easy to do with Mr. Ticks, who is a real physicist from MIT.

Mr. Ticks has twice attempted suicide, but found himself alive each time. He is unsure if he is the better for the experience. Mr. Ticks seeks the meaning of life and sometimes feels within the frustration of the moment the need to flip to the last page to find the answer. I feel that the next time Mr. Ticks turns the page he will find the answer.

"If you put enough cells in a row, you will have a thought process. What immortal hand framed the symmetry of cells bending to an unknown directive towards an unseen sun? If electrons do not think, what hides within this endless web of connections that gives birth to thought? The need for dark energy to explain the expanding universe is of little interest in relation to the need to know what lies between the building blocks of matter and energy to explain thought itself. Sometimes I feel I can almost touch this reality, and then it falls away from me as if it dared me to follow through the infinite tunnels of the mind. Sometimes I think I am just a thought within some other's mind."

You are right, Mr. Ticks, we are all just thoughts in some other's mind. In my mind are many thoughts like Mr. Ticks who spins his endless web of questions, for if we knew the answers there could never have been questions.

IDEAS OF REFERENCE

"I was arguing with my wife. I felt like knocking her teeth in because I knew she was right, and I was so drunk. To hell with it. I just decided I would get my clothes and get the hell out of there. I just packed a suitcase and told her she would never see me again even if she rode her broom all over the damn city. Then I remember my son standing in the corner of the room. "Papa, please don't go. I'll be better. I'll be a good boy. Don't take your clothes, Papa." That's what he said, that's what my five-year old son said, but I left him there. I left him there. He was so small, so tiny, and I left him there. I don't even know what I argued with my wife about, I was too drunk. I was so mad and I don't even know what I was mad about. I know I wanted some more to drink, and I wanted to see another woman, and I didn't want to be nagged about getting drunk. I know that. "Please, please don't go, Papa." I remember his hands holding the shoes that he can never tie and the tears on his cheeks. I see him standing there in the doorway, and I think I will never drink again; then I have another drink so I can forget about him standing there in the doorway. Christ, it just never ends."

Yes, it never ends. When you are a small child, ideas of reference are normal; you believe that events occur due to your actions, or lack of action, that really are not in reference to you or your behavior. The outside reality is of no importance for the child; his father leaves because the child is unworthy of the father staying or because of all the bad things the child has done. It is so sad and it lasts forever. Only bits and pieces can be changed, and their shadows linger in the corners of your mind.

"I hate myself for what I have done to the child. I can't change it though. I don't know if I can change anything." The child stands in the doorway holding his small shoes with the laces he cannot learn to tie and the broken heart and fear that washes into the night.

I know Mr. Ariosto, I know. I too have left so many small, crying beings in the doorways of the past. I will try to do better. And I have been left in the doorway crying too.

The Weeds of God   215

Somewhere, Mr. Ariosto, you are in the doorway and I must try to unravel what makes you run to hide in the sanctuary of drink. There are things we all must confront straight up in the face of the tiger with fear and dread. There is no place to hide. You must go out to do battle for the alternative is endless loathing of self.

Come, Mr. Ariosto, let us do battle. Each man is a coward for some things and on some days, but your fear can be overcome. We will walk towards the places where the tigers wait, and step through the glass, darkly spattered with terror as we near the tall grass waving gently with memories of battles lost. Look at the alternative and know this is all there is that can be real, the only battles that will ever matter. From where the sun now stands we will fight forever. This war never ends, and victory is only the knowledge that you will continue to persevere. *Nihil vos tenemus, patres conscripti.*

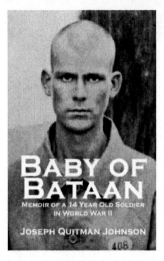

$25.00
Hardback • ISBN 1-59096-002-5

ForeWordreviews.com
The son, daughter, niece or nephew of someone you know was born in 1990. Picture him or her serving a tour of duty in Iraq or Afghanistan. If it seems impossible - how, after all, could someone that young get into the military at all? - you immediately understand why *Baby of Bataan* is so captivating.

Joseph Quitman Johnson was indeed all of 14 years old when he enlisted in the army shortly before America's entry into World War II. His experiences during that time, up to, and through the surrender of the Philippines to the Japanese, then through several years as a prisoner of war, comprise the vast bulk of the book.

Beyond the basic premise of a 14-year-old in the service, what's startling and, in the end, so inspirational is how much Johnson recollects and conveys - without editorializing, romanticizing, sentimentalizing, or fabricating - the perspective of war through a teenager's eyes. He makes it clear early on why he enlisted in the first place (family troubles) and spends the remainder of the book in a kind of soul-searching mode as he recounts the war's events and how, increasingly improbably, he survived.

You might say it was just dumb luck. Johnson recalls scene after scene in which he comes face to face with death; if it were a film, the ways in which fate seems to continually spare him would be considered so unlikely that the script would inevitably be rewritten. Johnson escapes the Bataan Death March and helps to fight at Corregidor until it surrenders. One moment he is being strafed by airplanes, in another he's tortured as a prisoner of war or on a "hell ship" commandeered by the Japanese which, after being hit by American bombing raids, starts to sink, forcing the GIs, starved and demoralized, to swim to shore. Over and over he rebounds from starvation, infection, broken bones, disease and depression - all the while learning to endure.

And endure he did. Johnson's memoir is not just a survey of his years in the Pacific theatre, but a coming-of-age tale under the worst possible circumstances. A panoply of characters - American, Filipino and Japanese - pass through the story, scores of them, and most of them he outlived. That such a memoir should unfold with such grace, valor and honesty in the writing is a testimonial to the men who fought beside Johnson and who, one could argue, died so he could live to tell the tale.

Online Review of Books

Imagine living a dozen action-packed, adventure-filled lifetimes in a period of five years. That's just what Joseph Quitman Johnson did and lived to tell about in his book, *Baby of Bataan: Memoir of a 14-Year-Old Soldier in World War II*, an incredible coming-of-age war memoir that is not only filled with extraordinary tales of bravery and survival, but also personalized in a way that makes it custom made for the silver screen.

The book is written as a first person narrative, and it recounts the true-life story of a young boy who grows up dirt poor in Memphis, Tennessee, and enlists in the army at the tender age of fourteen, pretending that he is 18. Sensing that the new recruit is actually younger than he claims, two older soldiers named Ray and Dale take Joe Johnson under their wings and introduce him to the ways of becoming a soldier during the pre-war days in the Philippines— from drinking his first beer to having his first sexual encounter.

During this time, Johnson falls in love with a young Filipino prostitute named Felicia, who becomes pregnant and is doomed to a life of hardship and misery. Filled with compassion for the young girl, Johnson steals her away from the brothel and brings her to a convent, where he pays for her first month's room and board and promises the nuns in charge he will continue to send money to them out of his monthly army salary.

Soon after he leaves Felicia, Johnson sees action in Corregidor and Bataan and recounts the horrors of war. Perhaps the most poignant episode in this phase of his life is the one in which he describes the death of one of his best friends:

"The juice tanks had been riddled with bullet holes, and juice was still dripping on an already saturated ground. It had spread over a large area and was drying in the dirt. We stopped short and stared at the bodies of the lieutenant and two soldiers who were lying sprawled in the middle of the drying juice, stripped of their equipment. Ray's body was propped against a juice tank, his head drooping against his chest. Large red fire ants covered his body. Then I realized that all the bodies were covered with the red fire ants, the ant's bright red shells were glistening in the sun. It was a sight that I would forever have etched in my mind."

But this is only the beginning of his nightmare. As the war continues, he and his other best friend, Dale, are captured and tortured in a Japanese prisoner of war camp. Dale attempts to escape, but he is captured and beheaded along with several other men. At this point Johnson realizes he is all alone and feels completely isolated and without hope. In addition to the daily tortures and humiliations, he describes how he is forced to work long hours with little to eat, and how he becomes sickly and loses weight:

"My health was deteriorating rapidly. The hard labor and the starvation diet with its lack of essential vitamins were taking their toll. I was suffering from dry beriberi, pellagra, scurvy, and now I had a bout of chronic diarrhea again. I had numerous large ulcers and open sores on my legs and ankles, which never seemed to heal."

If this weren't enough, Johnson endures even more hardships, including being beaten to within an inch of his life by a sadistic Japanese guard. Throughout it all, however, he never gives up and lives to see the end of the war. And even more remarkably, his story ends with a dramatic twist that rewards his courage and humanity in a way that even the best Hollywood screenwriter would applaud.

$16.00
Hardback • ISBN 1-59096-000-9

Midwest Book Review
An impressively written novel that vividly evokes a fictional yet highly
realistic memory of a Marine who served in combat in Vietnan. Offers the
reader a compellingly dark, gritty, no-holds-barred view of a truly hellish
war, and the toll it took on human life and decency. *Goodbye Vietnam*
belongs on the shelf alongside such seminal and memorable works as
Joseph Heller's *Catch 22* and Norman Mailer's *The Naked and the Dead*.

The Book Reader
Beautifully written. A compelling, quite splendid short study that comes as
close to capturing the real Vietnam War as any Socially Unacceptable
authenticity can.

Leatherneck Magazine
Like pieces of shrapnel; the words sting and they go deep.

ForeWordreviews.com
Five Stars. An exceptional book.
About a third of the way into Wood's fantastic Vietnam free-prose collection,
he ends "Unimportant," a short piece about the bloody defense of an insignifi-
cant bridge, with the words, "I have taken a picture."

In *Goodbye Vietnam,* Wood has created a series of snapshots of the absurdity of war in much the same way that Tim O'Brien did in his magnificent war idylls *If I Die in a Combat Zone, Box Me Up and Ship Me Home* and *The Things They Carried.* Similar to O'Brien, Wood has chosen the format of a loosely metered narrative described over the course of what are essentially sixty-two short-short stories. These stories range from less than a page to about three pages in length. The book opens with a dedication "To All Those We Left Behind" and ends with thirteen pages of responses to "Lies, Misconceptions, and Half-Truths" about the Vietnam conflict. The aggregate effect of these short glimpses of madness, violence, sex, and death is a breathless mélange of one soldier's descent into the darkness of war.

Though Wood occasionally betrays a classical education in his quoting of such things as Yeats's "The Second Coming" (in "Mom Calling": "What crawls my way from Bethlehem this night?"), the power of *Goodbye Vietnam* is in the visceral quality of its imagery and its emotional, absurdist rawness. Consider "The Cost of Little Boys" and its negotiation of the price to be paid to a grieving family whose child has been run over by an American military vehicle; or "Green Smoke Morning," which begins: "It's a green smoke morning. My feet are alive and screaming. My mouth is a crematorium for two million cigarettes."

Wood's work also evokes Tom Waits' hard-bitten lyricism on *Swordfishtrombone* in that it is uncompromising in its forcefully directed simplicity. The patterns of his word choice, the strength of repetition in such found phrasings as "hated-Cong" and "his cooler-than-you .45," combine into ritual - a kind of power through rhythm that marks the best of prosody and reportage alike.

Goodbye Vietnam is just as the title suggests, an exorcism of the demons of armed warfare through the brutal remembering of them. Wood's work is incandescent in its anger and brilliant in its ability to convey the importance of simple pleasures like tobacco, a cold can of Coke, and a package of cookies mailed from home to a frontline soldier who's been humping a 200-pound pack over most of Vietnam.

In a time in America's history when there is a renewed call to patriotism, *Goodbye Vietnam* will remind readers that even foot soldiers in unpopular conflicts deserve our gratitude for what they left behind in paddies not of their choosing. Robert Wood has created a thing of beauty and vigor.